High Plains Heartbreak

High Plains Heartbreak

Love on the High Plains: Book 3

Simone Beaudelaire

Contents

Prologue

Garden City, Kansas 1884

"Jes...se?" A broken voice penetrated Jesse West's focus for a brief moment. He lifted his head. The rarest of commodities, a gentle breeze warmed by a kind, late-April sun seemed to kiss the tears streaming unceasingly down his cheeks. Then his gaze dropped back to the raw mound of earth at his feet. All around him, under the partial shade of wind-blasted oaks, other freshly dug graves—too many of them—clawed the earth apart. He dropped his eyelids.

Warmth penetrated the shoulders of his shirt. He did not react to the touch except to murmur softly, "Kristina."

"Jesse, I'm so sorry. So sorry." The grip of her capable musician's hands became a full-bodied hug as she crushed him from behind. *She's so strong.*

But not strong enough to stem the flow of tears, or to stop his heart from bleeding. *Can a heart bleed to death?* He wondered idly, staring at a furrow in the upended soil. *Just bleed and die and leave a shell of a man who eats and breathes but isn't really alive?* "I wish it had been me."

"Oh, Jesse!" Kristina began to sob and her tears soaked into the back of his shirt.

Reluctantly he turned his back on the grave. *Not like it matters. She's with the angels now, not in the cold ground. It's not like I'll ever forget the sight.* "Kris, I..." his voice broke. It was just as well, as he had no idea what to say.

"I'm so sorry," Kristina sobbed again. "Lily was such a good girl. I was so happy for you both..."

Her words cut fresh lacerations in the bleeding wounds on his soul. *The best girl,* he replied silently. *Every man's dream of a woman. How could this happen? Tomorrow was supposed to be our wedding day!* The unfairness of life clogged Jesse's throat so badly he felt he could choke on it. *I wish I would.*

But here was one of his closest friends, standing five feet from her mother's equally fresh grave, trying to comfort him.

"I know, Kris. I..." He took a shuddering breath. "You're no better. Your poor mama..."

At his words she went completely to pieces, shuddering as she cried.

"Hey," he said, lifting her face so he could look into her ocean-green eyes. She had been so ravaged by grief, every inch of visible skin between her heavy freckles had tear stains. Her snub nose ran unchecked. He handed her a handkerchief. She wiped without the slightest attention, her eyes locked on his. "Kris, I'm sorry about your mama, but at least you'll be away from all this grief soon. You'll be glad to get back to school, won't you?"

She shook her head. "I'm not going."

Jesse's jaw dropped, the shock of her words cutting through his sorrow. "Kris, what?" His eyebrows drew together into a solid line. "You're the most talented musician I've ever known. How can you even consider not going back to the conservatory? How can you stay here in this gossip-factory of a town with all these memories?"

"I have to," she replied, her lip quivering. "I can't leave Dad alone."

"Cal can stay," Jesse insisted. *Let those two stallions battle it out. Cal can help at the general store.*

"Cal left. When we woke up this morning, he was gone. Left a note on the table." Her full lips, her prettiest feature after her eyes, twisted into a wry parody of a grin. "He said he'd had enough of Dad's bossy ways, and with Mom gone he was going to seek his fortune." She sniffled.

Why that little... "I'm sorry, Kris."

This time, the pain lashed her features.

Poor Kris. With those freckles, who knows if she'll ever find a husband? And then to lose her career too. Life's unfair. At the thought of just how unfair, another tear escaped him, trailing down his wind burned cheek and moistening his stubble.

"You should go back anyway," he told her with brutal honesty. "Go and live, Kris. You can't stay here. This town is a dead end. You'll never have a future here. Go and finish school and play your music all over. Don't let your dreams die."

"I can't." Desolate despair weighed down her pugnacious features into the caricature of a bulldog. "But at least I'll have my friends around me." Her turquoise eyes seemed to plead. *I know what she wants—what she'd never admit to, standing here over Lily's grave—but it won't be. I can't marry Kristina. I don't love her enough, and that's worse than being alone.*

Slowly, his soul burning as badly as his eyes, he drove another nail into the coffin of her future. "Not me. I'm leaving in the morning. I don't think I'll ever come back."

Part I

Chapter 1

Eastern Colorado 1889

The San Juan Mountains thrust heavenward, snowcapped despite the uncertain warmth of March, clustered below a fiery sunset. In the waning light, the rocky peaks had darkened from their usual blue to nearly a purple tone. On the prairie below, a lone rider atop a silver horse galloped toward the massed rock formations of the foothills. Under his breath he muttered one prayer after another to a God he no longer respected, begging for time... more time... *Please, God, let me be in time!*

He crested the first hill at a dangerous speed, his horse's iron shoes clattering and slipping on the loose gravel. Mercury snorted in protest, and despite his hurry the rider patted his mount's neck and reined in, slowing the pace. *I can't do a lick of good if I kill myself and my horse along the way.* And still, the litany repeated unceasingly in the back of his mind. *Please let me arrive in time. Please more time. I need a bit more time...*

Time was against him, and every metallic clang of horseshoes on rock sounded like the ticking of a clock counting down the hours... the hours of his best friend's life. *Death has been too hard on me.* Jesse blinked against the sudden sting in his eyes. A crusty old bounty hunter like Clevis McCoy would not want to be remembered with tears. *Most likely with a slug of moonshine and a pistol salute... I can arrange that.* Clev wasn't dead yet. *Please. God, let him not be dead yet. Not before I say goodbye... and deal with the urgent business he mentioned in the telegram.*

Mercury stumbled and righted himself again. Jesse reigned in a bit tighter. The sun had slipped further behind the mountains, under which Jesse now struggled to see enough to move forward safely. *Damned old man. Why did he wait until the last minute? I came as soon as I could... couldn't turn loose a bail jumper... not even for this. He knew that. Hell, he taught me that. No time. No time.*

From over the next hill, a skinny finger of smoke rose towards the burnished and cloud-clustered sky. *Those look like thunderheads. Damn it, the last thing I need is rain too.*

But Jesse had no wood to knock, and the unwanted rain obligingly began to pour over him, sluicing out of the folds of his black hat in a stream that could hardly obscure his vision more than the sudden veil of droplets between him and his destination. Mercury whickered a complaint as the soil under his hooves transformed into mud.

"Sorry, buddy," Jesse muttered. "Sorry. We'll be there soon. Few minutes is all."

Mercury, it seemed, was unconvinced by Jesse's reassurance. He continued to mutter and sulk in his equine displeasure with every step.

The slow trek over the hill and into the shaded valley seemed to take a hundred years, what with the rain and the growing darkness, and the horse's tendency to balk, but in the end, the man and mount clattered up to the front door of a stone cottage nestled between two fat pines at the base of a cliff.

Wrapping the reins around one of the pillars that supported the roof of the porch, Jesse stomped up the wooden stairs, water sloshing uncomfortably inside his boots, and knocked on the unfinished pine door. A thick splinter embedded itself in his hand, but he ignored the sting, focused on gaining entry into the house as quickly as he could.

Slowly the door swung inward and Jesse strode forward, scarcely taking in the slight, high-cheekboned, red-haired female form beside him, but offering a cursory tip of his sodden hat, more by rote than out of any sense of courtesy.

The familiar structure spread out before him, illuminated by a crackling golden fire that served to dispel the chill of the early spring rain. The large room consisted of a stove and table to his left, wooden-armed sofa and rough-hewn rocking chair to his right. Beside the rocker, a closed door led to an addition that contained only Addie's single, tiny bedroom. Beyond the sofa, behind a curtain, the sound of fitful wheezing filtered through to Jesse's straining ears. He released a shaky breath. *Not too late.*

"Mr. West?" A soft voice, its normally soothing tone stained with grief and stress, emerged from the figure beside him.

He glanced. The fiery-haired young woman regarded him with a look he recognized in her big brown eyes. *I know that look of impending grief all too well.* "Yes, Miss McCoy?"

"Want me to stable your horse?"

Normally Jesse would have declined the offer. He preferred to care for his horse himself, being a meticulous type. Besides, Mercury could be unpredictable, though Adeline McCoy seemed to have inherited unusual horse sense–along with her striking cheekbones and dark eyes–from her deceased Kiowa mother. *Now, she's about to lose her father, too. Poor little mite.*

Jesse wondered, not for the first time, how old the girl was. While tiny in stature, a hint of curves under her homespun calico dress hinted at growing maturity. *Fourteen? Fifteen? Surely no older.* He shrugged. *You're stalling. You nearly broke your neck getting here. Don't delay. She's a smart, sensitive girl. She can handle Mercury for a few minutes.* Suppressing a twinge of guilt at sending the child out in the pouring rain, Jesse answered her, "I'd sure appreciate it if you would, Miss McCoy."

She nodded, relief in her eyes at the thought of something constructive to do, wrapped a shawl over the bright beacon of her auburn hair and slipped out the door. Her feet, bare despite the cold, made no sound on the floorboards. Jesse gulped, took a deep breath and moved across the room to the curtain. With every step, reality seemed to fade until he could have sworn he was floating. His feet felt numb. His breathing grew shallower with every step until lack of oxygen contributed to his overall dizziness. Reaching the rear wall of the cabin, he laid a hand on the board. The sting of his un-dealt with splinter served to wake him up with a jolt.

"Clev?" he called through the curtain.

The response was a tortured groan. Jesse pulled back the curtain and his heart clenched. The man who lay prone on the stained and foul-smelling bed bore little resemblance to his years' long friend. Only the gunmetal grizzle on the sagging jowls and the intelligent blue eyes revealed the man who had once been Colorado's most successful bounty hunter. The rest of him had been rendered unrecognizable by the slow, agonizing process of the disease on his body. *Consumption.* The deterioration of the lungs, accompanied by sweating, weight loss, and eventually coughing up blood. *I'll never forget the day he told me. He stood as strong as ever, but there was fear in his eyes. It's no surprise He'd stared down the barrel of a gun, and into the maw of a rattlesnake, and never flinched. It wasn't the death he feared, but the dying.*

"Jess…" the man wheezed. Then his attempt to speak dissolved into a fit of coughing that ended in a mouthful of red saliva being deposited into a filthy handkerchief. Jesse swallowed so he wouldn't gag at the sight.

"I'm here now, Clev," Jesse told his friend. "I made it like I promised."

Clevis gasped, trying to draw air into what was left of his lungs. His face turned even paler and his lips took on a bluish tint. Jesse watched in alarm, not sure what, if anything, he could do to help, and whether his friend was going to expire on the spot, without uttering another word.

Finally, the gasping subsided. Clevis gave a tremendous wheeze and fell back, exhausted, against the pillows. "Jesse," he whispered. "I'm glad you're here. Won't be… long now."

Jesse nodded. There was no point in denying the obvious. "You said you needed me to do something for you. What was it?" Jesse cringed. If merely articulating his name had nearly brought about Clevis' demise, how could he explain what kind of favor he wanted? But instead of speaking, Clev waved toward his bureau, set at the foot of his bed. Jesse noticed a slip of paper sitting on top.

Glad for something new to concentrate on, he retrieved the scrap, trying hard to ignore the pinkish fingerprints in the margins, and read.

Dear Jesse,

Whether you make it in time to see me off or not is no great matter. I know how life keeps a person running. I won't hold it against you, but either way, I need you to do something for me. My daughter, Addie, can't stay here. It's too isolated with me gone. Not to mention, there's some mealy-mouthed preacher from town who wants to marry my girl and won't take no for an answer.

Marry her? Jesse shook his head. Mountain people never ceased to amaze him. Addie was far too young to take a husband. He returned to reading.

I need you to take my girl to my sister in Colorado Springs. Beth McCoy. She's promised to care for Addie until a husband comes along.

Awareness dawned on Jesse that he might have underestimated the girl's age a bit.

I know it won't take long, pretty as she is, but she's a spitfire too. Like her mama.

Jesse could hear the old man's dry chuckle as he read the line. He'd always liked smart, strong women, even if it was only for the night.

So that's the favor I needed. Take my Addie to my sister. I have nothing to offer in exchange, but I trust our friendship is reason enough.

Jesse nodded. *More than enough, old man.*

He set the letter back on the bureau. His skin was crawling and he felt the urge to scrub his fingers with lye soap and hot water. Lacking that option, he rubbed vigorously on his damp jeans and hoped for the best. "Of course I'll do it."

If possible, Clevis' already limp body seemed to sag even more. "Thank..." he wheezed and then cut off and took two deep, labored breaths.

"You're welcome. Rest, friend. I know you're tired. Rest."

Clevis dipped his chin and closed his eyes. When lying still, he seemed better able to control his breathing. There was something wet about the sound, and it chilled Jesse to the core to listen to it.

Standing awkwardly beside his friend, wanting to be present, but not too close for fear of contagion, Jesse's thoughts spun in endless, pointless circles.

Into the maelstrom penetrated a soft sound. The door swung open on a creaky hinge and wet, bare feet slapped on the floorboards.

A moment later, Jesse jumped as an icy hand slipped into his. He turned his eyes away from the tableau of death before him and took in the slight figure of Adeline McCoy, who was regarding him with an unreadable expression in her eyes. She had never touched him before, and he wondered at her doing it now. His question must have been obvious because she breathed, "He won't let me near him."

"Too right, girl," Clevis choked. "I won't have you catching this damned..." he broke off, not in a cough, but in a choke. Adeline stepped forward, but he waved her back with a violent chop of his hand. Jesse tightened his grip, not allowing her to approach as Clevis' choking continued, accompanied by vile gagging and a dribble of bloody saliva running down his chin.

Clev's flailing hand clenched into a fist as he struggled to draw air into his diseased lungs. The blue tint to his lips spread to his chin and the skin under his nose, matching it to his stubble. Panic flared in his eyes and his hands went to his chest, clawing and clutching at the loose white nightshirt he wore.

Addie yanked hard on Jesse's hand. He retaliated with a sharp tug, twirling her into a crushing hold that was half hug, half restraint, her back pressed against his chest. She stared, mute but tense as a bowstring, her whole body trembling. The more Clevis struggled to draw air, the less he seemed to get. His skin turned ashen as he flailed and finally went limp, a thin rivulet of blood trickling from the side of his mouth.

"Nooooo!" Addie screamed, trying to wrench herself from Jesse's grip. He held on tight.

"Hush now," he urged. "Hush. I don't know if it's safe to go near him."

"He's my papa," she wailed, thrashing in his arms.

"I know. He loved you a whole lot. He wouldn't want you to risk getting sick. That's why he wouldn't let you near him. Don't waste his sacrifice. Be still."

Whether Jesse's words made sense to the hysterical girl or she simply lost her will to fight, he didn't know, but she turned, burying her face in his shirt and sobbing.

When he was certain she wouldn't approach her father's body, he relaxed a bit, his hold turning to a hug. He patted her back while she soaked the white linen with tears. With no end in sight and no reason to suspect any would be forthcoming, Jesse lifted the girl into his arms. Again the thought crossed his mind that she must be older than he'd believed. Despite her diminutive size, her weight was greater than he'd expected, as though a multitude of feminine curves were concealed under her dowdy dress. He carried her to the rough-hewn sofa and sank onto the rawhide upholstery. They'd made it themselves, the two of them, he recalled.

His own heart aching, Jesse cradled Addie on his lap until sleep overtook them both.

Chapter 2

"What will happen now?"

Jesse opened his eyes and groaned. His neck felt as though Mercury had been sitting on it. Sun blasted through the windows, stinging his eyes so he had to squint to see Addie standing before him, extending a cup of coffee. He accepted it gratefully, taking a sip of the scalding liquid as he blinked several times trying to clear away the scratchy, dry sensation. He felt like he'd been pushed, face-first, into a pile of red ants.

As he woke up, he thought about how to answer her question. There were practical concerns. The doctor needed to come up. There would need to be arrangements made with the pastor and the undertaker. Thank the Lord it wasn't the height of summer, but Clevis McCoy's mortal remains wouldn't stay fresh forever, and so they needed to get to work right away.

"Now, Miz McCoy? Once we deal with… everything, I'm taking you to your aunt in Colorado Springs. Your papa asked me to."

She blinked. "No. This is my home. Why would I want to go to Colorado Springs? I don't know anyone there. I barely know my aunt."

"Think," he replied, trying to snap her out of her confusion with a harsh tone. "You're just a young girl. You can't stay here by yourself. Anything could happen to you. Without your father's income, what will you live on? Not to mention the danger!"

She said nothing. It struck him how incongruous her calmness seemed, especially after last night. The girl had just lost her father. Shouldn't she be sad? He regarded her closely. While there was a bruised, grieving look to her brown eyes, her chiseled face was set, stoic. She resembled her father more in that moment than she ever had before. There was a stillness about her, a sense of accepting her grief rather than fighting it. *I wonder if that's something she learned from her mother.* He recalled when Clevis had learned his wife, whom he called Daisy because he couldn't pronounce her Kiowa name, had died while the two of them were tracking a murderer through the mountains. It was the only time Jesse had ever seen Clev cry.

And now he's gone. The sandpaper feeling of Jesse's eyes turned to a familiar sting. *Don't let go of it, Jesse. Hold yourself together. Clev wouldn't want that kind of tribute.* Not to mention how embarrassing it would be to go all to pieces while the girl in front of him didn't.

Addie stared into his eyes and he blinked twice to clear his vision.

"How old are you?" he blurted suddenly. His cheeks began to burn at the rudeness of the question.

"Nineteen," she replied succinctly, unembarrassed by his impertinence.

Now it was Jesse's turn to blink in disbelief. *Nineteen? An adult? No wonder her dad was talking about her finding a husband.* "Oh," he said stupidly. Then, to cover his awkwardness, he stood and stretched, groaning again as his neck popped loudly. "Should we go down to town and see about finding the doctor and the minister?"

The abrupt question brought them back to the present and the awareness of their crushing grief. Just behind the curtain lay the body of a man they'd both cared for. A body that would need to be cleaned and buried, prayed over and finally left behind, with no one to visit his grave.

This time it was Addie whose eyes shone with tears. Her lip trembled. Jesse gripped her shoulder, trying to bring her a small measure of comfort. "You're not alone, Addie," he mumbled.

She nodded, her breath catching on a deep inhalation before she stepped away from Jesse. "Do you want any breakfast?"

"No thanks," he replied. "I'm not hungry. When you're ready, shall we head to town?"

She nodded. "I'm not hungry either."

"Can you ride?" he asked, hoping Mercury would allow it. Normally the horse balked at anyone other than him on his back. "I don't have a sidesaddle."

Addie froze and turned, staring at him, the full rosebud of her lower lip drooping slightly open. "Sidesaddle? Sacrilege. Do you honestly think either of my parents would ever have permitted me to use one?"

Jesse, who had just taken in a mouthful of coffee, swallowed quickly to avoid choking on it. *Humor even now? What spirit this girl has.*

He smiled sadly. *Clev must have been so proud of her.* No, that was wrong. Jesse was no longer clear on what he believed about anything, but he had no doubt that somewhere, right now, his friend was looking down at his daughter and smiling. "Point taken," he said. "Get some shoes on and let's get moving."

"I hate shoes," Addie replied, but she consented to stick her feet into a pair of men's boots anyway. *Or rather boy's boots,* Jesse thought with amusement. *No man ever had feet that small.*

As Addie busied herself getting ready for the ride, Jesse opened every window he could find in the cabin. While the wind in the mountains blew much less intensely than in his prairie hometown, he hoped it would be enough to dispel any contagion lingering around the room. Then he proceeded to the lean-to which housed the McCoy family's ancient, swaybacked mule, their milk cow and half a dozen chickens. *Wait, what happened to Stormy?* Sure enough, Clev's gelding was nowhere to be seen. The stall in which Mercury stood should not have been empty. *Must have gotten rid of him, once he got too sick to work.*

A chilly breeze reminded Jesse of the inclement weather. The unhappy chickens clustered together in a patch of sunshine, their feathers fluffed. *I wonder how they keep the birds warm in the winter... I wonder what will become of them.*

He slipped Mercury's bridle into place and led him out of the makeshift stall where he'd spent the night. The gelding leveled a sour look at the sorry-looking structure and tossed his glistening mane. Shabby housing or not, Mercury had been well groomed. Jesse regarded the saddle. The trip into town—if the unincorporated collection of buildings around the Pagosa Hot Springs could be called a town—would take the best part of an hour on foot, which would be their only means of transportation since the old mule hardly looked able to meander across the meadow, let alone carry anyone. Though the sun shone brightly on the still-damp grass and pale green shoots that would someday become spring flowers, another chilly breeze ruffled Jesse's hair and shot straight through his shirt. He shivered.

The sound of dry grass crackling drew his attention to his left, where Addie approached, dressed in an oversized leather coat he'd seen many times. He looked askance at the girl, one blond eyebrow raised. She shrugged, making the heavy fabric creak, and turned to Mercury. The horse whickered a greeting, clearly having forgiven her for putting him in the hated barn. She approached without a hint of fear and stroked his velvety nose for a moment before circling around. Jesse turned to retrieve the saddle from the rear of the storage area which formed the right-hand side of the 'barn'. A sudden noise snared his attention and he turned, startled to find Addie sitting astride the barebacked horse, her legs hanging down over his flanks. Jesse's jaw dropped. "But... the saddle?"

She shrugged. It seemed to be her signature gesture. "That's the sissy way. I don't need it. Besides, it's not big enough for both of us."

He blinked. "I thought I'd walk."

"Walk? With this strong boy standing by?" She patted the horse's neck. "He can carry us both to town. Hop on, Mr. West."

His formal name sounded wrong on her lips. Though he'd seen her a few times over the years, they'd never exactly known each other well enough to be friends, and yet...

"Call me Jesse," he said gruffly as he vaulted onto the horse's back. *Damn, this is hard without stirrups.* Seizing the reigns, he turned the horse towards the township of Pagosa Springs.

"All right, Jesse," Addie said, her voice so soft the breeze threatened to carry it away. With her body pressed close to his, he became far more aware of her warmth and the softness of her curves than he would really have liked. "I never much cared for the Miss and Mister business anyway. What purpose does it serve to create distance?"

This time Jesse shrugged. "It's just the way it's done, Addie." After all, she'd just said, calling her Miz McCoy again made no sense.

"Not good enough. I like to know the reason for something before I do it."

"There isn't always a reason, Addie, except to stay out of trouble," he said patiently. *She's still so young.*

"People see me and automatically assume I'm trouble," she replied. "At least if they knew my mother."

"Are they right?" he asked, an impish smile playing around his mouth as his eyes scanned the horizon. Or at least what he could see before the view was interrupted by blue mountain peaks capped in white. Before them, pine trees crowded close, their fragrance perfuming the gentle breeze. *This is so unlike Kansas.* Something about the mountains and trees never failed to make Jesse feel unsettled. Growing up in the middle of an unending prairie, able to see the horizon in all directions, the wind constantly in his ears, all the obstructions made him feel closed in.

"You're tense. What's wrong?" the girl asked.

I'm not about to admit to her that mountains make me edgy. "I'm heading into a town I don't know, to meet with people I don't know to plan my best friend's funeral."

"You don't need to," she replied. "Dad made all the arrangements weeks ago. We only need to let the appropriate people know."

Of course. That fits perfectly. Scared or not, Clev couldn't have faced death with anything less than the strength and preparedness with which he embraced life.

Addie's shoulders trembled. *Poor girl. She's trying so hard to be strong, but she's basically alone in the world. Must be terrifying.*

Her fear and loneliness resonated with Jesse. He knew exactly what she was feeling. As the gentle rhythm of the horse's hooves and the sweet scent of pine washed over them, some of their tension melted away.

"Do you know the first time I met your dad?" he asked.

She moved her head in a 'no' fashion.

"I was in jail." Jesse chuckled at the memory.

"What did you do?" her voice, soft and curious, filtered back to him.

"I got drunk. Then I cheated at cards. Then I got in a fight. I thought they were going to string me up, but as hung-over as I was, it seemed like a pretty good idea. Your dad stepped in and pointed out that I hadn't taken anyone's money, and a couple of broken barstools was a pretty small crime to stretch a boy's neck for. I was just your age at the time."

She didn't reply, but he knew she was listening. There was a sense of alertness in her silence.

"He bailed me out and convinced the owner of the bar I busted up to exchange a couple weeks' work for his troubles since I didn't have any money. Your dad stayed around to make sure I paid off my debts and then dragged me out of town and taught me how to do honest work."

"He always was a hero," she said, and Jesse detected a hint of irony in her voice.

"A hero to everyone else, huh?"

"Yes," she replied, and then a little sob escaped. "Damn it."

Jesse raised his eyebrows at the curse. "Not much of a lady, are you?"

She chuckled, though her breathing was far from steady. "No, not at all."

"Good," he replied. "Then I won't have to worry about offending you with my coarse, bounty hunter ways."

She laughed again, a little more convincingly this time. "What do you think my dad was? I learned a lot from him when he was home. Jesse…" she broke off.

"What is it, Addie?"

"We're here talking and laughing about Dad. He… he passed yesterday. Is it wrong?"

Jesse thought about her question. "No," he replied. "I don't think so. I mean, I knew him pretty well. I think he'd like that we're remembering him with laughter rather than tears."

"Or at least only tears," she added, wiping her eyes.

"He was an unconventional man. We'll mourn him and remember him in the way that's most fitting, agreed?"

"Agreed."

They lapsed into silence.

All the long way into town a warm sun shone on their shoulders and heads while the cold nibbled their fingers and noses. At last, the town came into view. A small collection of flat-fronted, two-story buildings painted garish colors fronted a large body of water. A few pioneer homes dotted the landscape nearby.

Addie directed Jesse down the path to the one cobblestone street, turning left and following the shore along its edge to a tall, slender wooden structure painted gleaming white with brown trim, tucked into the shadow of a great Ponderosa pine. A wooden cross over the entryway identified the building.

Without waiting for Mercury to stop, Addie slid from the back of the horse and ran to the door, knocking twice and then opening. By the time Jesse had wrapped Mercury's reins around the church's support pillar and climbed the rickety wooden steps into the one-room structure, Addie had found her way to the front and was sitting beside the pastor, a gentleman of indeterminate years with silver threads in his dark hair and a smooth, unlined face. He grasped Addie's hands gently in both of his, Jesse saw as he reached them.

This must be the mealy-mouth Clev disliked so much. Though to be honest, the pastor didn't seem like such a bad guy. He clearly cared about Addie. She, on the other hand, had the stiff shoulders and frozen expression of someone who isn't comfortable. She nodded politely at the pastor's soothing words but didn't seem connected to them.

"Reverend," Jesse said, breaking through the conversation.

Both faces turned to him and he saw a flash of relief in Addie's eyes.

"Hello there. I'm Pastor Joseph Allen. You can call me Joe."

"Jesse West." Jesse extended his hand, which forced the pastor to release Addie so he could turn around and shake.

He met the girl's eyes over the top of the man's head and she raised her eyebrows. Jesse schooled his face into stillness. He doubted Miss Adeline McCoy would have been swayed in the slightest by this man's attempts to woo her.

"Pleased to meet you, Jesse," the reverend said. "Are you a relative of the McCoys?"

"Just a family friend," he replied, switching his speech to the more proper patterns he'd learned as a child. "Miss McCoy informs me that her father has already made arrangements for his funeral and burial?"

"Yes indeed," the pastor replied, rising to his feet. Addie also stood, and the three stepped into the aisle. While two people could converse comfortably in a church pew, a trio in that configuration would mean someone always had their back to someone else. Jesse had to suppress another grin when he realized the pastor was only a bit taller than Addie. *Hope he makes up for his size with some fiery sermons and fist pounding.*

"So what's the plan then?" Jesse asked.

"Once the doctor," Reverend Joe made a face, "has done... what he needs to do, Mr. McCoy requested an immediate burial with only a small service to mark it. I can have everything arranged by tomorrow. Can you two have Mr. McCoy ready by then?"

Jesse gulped. He'd forgotten that the burden of washing and dressing Clev would fall on them. "Only if the doctor agrees it's safe."

Addie made a face at him, one which clearly labeled him a sissy.

So be it. Like Clev, I'm not afraid of dying, but slowly choking for years isn't the way I want to go. Giving the girl a quick eyebrow gesture, he returned his attention to the pastor, who was regarding them both with a curious expression.

"Of course," the little man agreed. "No one wants to start an epidemic. So far, consumption has more or less passed us by, except for poor Mr. McCoy, of course. We'd like to keep it that way."

"So it will be a small, simple service then?"

"Yes," Addie replied. "Dad didn't have much use for preachers, as you know." She sent Joe one of her silent looks, this one clearly an apology. He acknowledged the gesture with a wry twisting of his lips. The pastor smoothed his dark hair with his fingertips as Addie continued. "He only wanted, as he said, 'a prayer said, a song sung, and some good food eaten.'"

"That sounds like him," Jesse commented. "I'm not the least bit surprised."

Addie dipped her chin, acknowledging his comment.

I like this girl, Jesse thought to himself. *I like her quiet ways.*

"And he spoke to the pianist, a lady who knows how to cook really well, and me," Pastor Joe added. "As well as the undertaker and the doctor. Basically, all you have to do is make sure Mr. McCoy is ready for the funeral."

The mention of a pianist brought to mind Kristina. It had been so long since he'd even written her a letter. *I wonder if Addie knows anything about music. I wonder why, having known her father so long, having eaten so many meals across the table from her, I know so little about her.* He tried to meet the girl's eyes again, but she was staring at the floor.

Realizing there was nothing left to say, Jesse wrapped up the conversation with the pastor quickly and ushered Addie out the door.

"How are you holding up?" he asked her.

She glanced his way for a moment and then looked down again, studying the dirt between the cobblestones with great intensity. "About as well as you'd expect," she replied. "Sometimes I want to cry, and other times I feel like laughing, though I can't understand why I would."

"All mixed up," he replied. "That's how it is. Shock, hysteria, and just plain grief. Let it play out the way it wants to, Addie. Don't kick yourself for feeling all muddled. That's normal."

"How do you know so much about it?" she asked, finally looking into his eyes again. Though she hadn't cried recently, the brown irises were rimmed with red. "You can't be much older than me."

"I'm twenty-five," he replied. "I've lost my share of loved ones in that time." A sudden memory floated up in his mind, of the cholera outbreak that had claimed so many just before he left Garden City for good. Of his own sweet Lily, now four... no, five years under the earth. His breath caught. Biting down on the inside of his cheek until he tasted blood, he counted slowly to fifty before he continued. "Loss is part of life."

"I hate it," Addie replied, and this time tears shimmered and one slipped down over her sculpted cheekbone. Angrily she dashed it away with her free hand. "I hate hurting like this. First Mama and now Papa." She shook her head.

"Hey, now," he said, pausing in the middle of the street and turning to face her, grasping both her arms in his hands. She looked up into his face. "I know you must be overwhelmed, Addie, but you'll get through this. You must be one of the strongest women I've ever met."

"I don't feel strong," she replied, her lip trembling, "and I don't want to break down in the middle of the street. Come on." She shook off his grip and grabbed his hand in hers, all but dragging him across to a small, one-story structure that nearly disappeared between a saloon with a girl in fancy knickers hanging over the balcony waving and calling the men who were passing in the street, and a hotel from which the smell of overcooked eggs wafted out horribly, mingling with the sulfur stench of the hot springs and the zephyr of pines on the mountainside.

Inside, the building proved to be a pocket-sized hospital with two high beds and a small desk behind which a white-haired man labored feverishly over a sheaf of papers. At the sound of boots on the wooden floor, he looked up, taking in his guests.

"Miss McCoy, does your father need me?" He rose to his feet.

She shook her head slowly from one side to the other. "Not anymore," she replied.

He bowed his head, acknowledging the meaning behind her words. "I know what you need then," he said at last. "I'll fill out... all the paperwork. I'm very sorry, Miss McCoy."

She swallowed and managed a watery smile.

"Just let me finish up this one thing," he waved a careless hand at the pile of papers on his desk, "and I'll be up there. Shouldn't be more than an hour or two."

"Is it... safe to be near him?" Jesse demanded.

The doctor crooked one bushy white eyebrow at him. "Yes, son. It's surprisingly hard to catch consumption. Just keep the windows open... and wash your hands. That can't hurt."

Jesse felt somewhat less than reassured by this, but the time for delaying had come to an end. Escorting a sniffling Adeline McCoy back into the street, he noticed with a start that quite a crowd of young men had gathered in front of the church. They seemed to be admiring Mercury.

"Gentlemen," Jesse said in a carrying voice as he approached the gelding. Several of the gathered group turned, and he saw they mostly seemed to be in their late teens. About Addie's age. He wondered if she would introduce him. Instead, the intrepid girl seemed to shrink at the sight of these youths. She slunk behind Jesse.

"What did you need, sir?" one of the boys, a blond in ragged trousers, asked. He seemed not to have noticed Addie.

"I just wanted to be sure everything was all right with my horse," Jesse replied. "You fellows seem mighty interested."

"He's a beaut!" a red-headed boy exclaimed his voice filled with awe. The freckles on his chubby cheeks seemed to be dancing with excitement.

"Thanks," Jesse said wryly, suddenly feeling old. He respected and cared for Mercury as though the horse were a trusted friend more than a work animal, but he couldn't remember the last time he'd been that excited over a mount. *Probably before all your hope died.*

"Wah-hoo!" A drawling voice hollered from behind him. Another, larger boy drew Jesse's attention as he yanked a small, familiar figure into view. Addie fought the bully with everything she had, scratching and biting, but his grip on her arm remained unbroken. "Look, fellas! It's the half-breed. Who wants a kiss? Pucker up, sweetheart."

"Let her go!" Jesse insisted, stepping forward and crowding into the bully's space, shoving him hard in the center of the chest. Once distracted, Jesse had no trouble wrenching Addie's slender wrist free.

She turned her back to the bully and kicked hard like a mule, her boot connecting with his knee. He howled and fell to the ground. Addie stood over him, her chest heaving, her hair flying loose from its burnished braid. "What did I tell you, Ed? What did I say I would do if you ever touched me again?" Without another word, she drove the toe of her boot into his groin with a force that had even Jesse wincing.

"Slut!" the boy named Ed wheezed. "You're so brave now that you have a man looking out for you. He'll leave you knocked up in a whorehouse somewhere…" the rest of the boy's words were not fit to repeat.

The other boys were starting to press forward, hoping to see more trouble. Jesse pushed past them and quickly unwound Mercury's reins from the post, climbing onto the church step before vaulting onto the horse's back. Kicking in gently with his heels, he urged his mount forward, scattering the adolescents.

Holding on tight with his knees, he leaned over and hooked one arm around Addie's waist, hauling her across his lap. As soon as her weight stabilized, he urged Mercury into a trot and then a gallop, not running hell-bent for leather, but making good time out of the town and back up to the safety of the mountains.

Once they cleared the last of the structures, he slowed the horse to a trot. At last, Addie managed to right herself, sitting up in the vee between his legs.

"What the hell just happened?" he asked.

"Ed Silver," she replied, as though that explained anything at all.

"And Ed Silver is?"

"Someone I wish I'd never known." She drew in a deep, shuddering breath.

Jesse leaned his chin on the top of her head. "Are you all right?"

"Yes," she replied, exhaling on a sigh.

"And you were going to argue with me," he pointed out, "about going to live with your aunt. What would you do, up there on that mountain alone, if that fellow decided he wanted another taste of you? You weren't holding your own too well against him."

Addie snorted. "I hadn't really started to fight yet. You'd be surprised what I can do, Jesse."

"Oh yeah?" he raised one eyebrow. "Like what?"

"You mean apart from riding bareback? I can shoot a gun better than many men, I can throw knives with good accuracy, and I know fighting techniques that use my size as an advantage."

Jesse shuddered again, remembering the hard kick she had delivered to that boy. *He deserved it, but ouch!* "You have to sleep sometimes," he pointed out. "What will you do if you wake up pinned down to the bed by three or four armed men twice your size?"

Addie's shoulders stiffened. She didn't answer, but he had the feeling she was more sulking than holding out hope of staying alone in that remote cabin.

By the time they arrived, Jesse's mind had turned back to the unpleasant task ahead of them. He didn't exactly trust the doctor's assurances that the contagion would be difficult to catch, and he knew the sight of his friend choking to death would stay with him for a long time.

Chapter 3

That evening, Jesse sat beside the roaring bonfire where the soiled bed linens and mattress on which Clevis McCoy had expired were being consigned to ash. His hands still stung from the long wash in lye soap and scalding water to which he'd treated them after helping Addie prepare her father's body for burial.

Though normally women's work, he'd lent a hand, knowing Addie had no one else. Certainly, none of the women from the town had hurried up the mountain to help the orphan with her task. So it had fallen to Jesse. At first, he'd feared Addie would lose her composure again, but apart from the slow tears meandering down her cheeks, she'd remained calm.

Now she sat beside him, cross-legged in front of the fire, weeping softly into a handkerchief. It felt natural for him to lay one arm across her shoulders, so he did. She inched closer. He hugged her tighter and then dared to drop a gentle kiss on the top of her head. "It'll be all right, Addie," he murmured. "You'll see. Everything will be just fine."

"Was it for you?" she asked.

"What do you mean?"

"You told me you had lost people you cared about. Were you just fine?"

Damn, this girl is perceptive. "All right, you got me. It's true, nothing is the same when someone you love dies. You never go back to the way you were, but, Addie, that doesn't mean your life is over, or that you will never feel happy again. Your life isn't over. It's just changing." As he spoke, his eyes never left the fire. It crackled and snapped, pouring warmth over the autumnal chill in the meadow. Addie also felt warm against his side. Warm and alive. Her spirit, though wounded by the specter of death hanging over them, remained unvanquished.

"Thank you for being honest," she said. "Are we really leaving the day after tomorrow?"

"Yeah," he replied, inhaling a fragrant waft of wood smoke and distant pines, of meadow grass and rotting leaves. "I think it's best if we do. It will take the best part of two weeks to get to Colorado Springs, and we don't want to be traveling on horseback if any mountain snowstorms hit. Besides, if I don't get back to work soon, I'll run out of money."

"I'll help, you out," she replied. "It's the least I can do. You can have part of the money from the sale of my property."

He shook his head. "It was lucky that fellow from town offered to buy up the place from you, including the animals, but he didn't pay you enough by half. That's your dowry, Miss Addie, and your lifeline. If anything happens, you'll need that money to live on. It's much easier for me to find honest work than you."

She responded to his words with a slow dip of the chin.

Morning found the two bereaved souls seated in a pew at the little church, regarding the gray, waxy-looking face of Clevis McCoy. Addie, it seemed, had cried herself out. She stared straight ahead, her expression far away. Today it was Jesse who struggled to contain his emotions. His eyes burned and he kept his handkerchief clutched in his fist, frequently wiping at his nose and silently cursing his fair coloring that turned red so easily around the eyes and nose.

Uncomfortable looking at the mortal remains of his friend, Jesse scanned the room instead. A simple church for a simple town, this one consisted only of two rows of pews, he guessed it totaled seating for about fifty, with a simple rail up front with a pulpit in it, and a piano on the left-hand side. *Not much to look at,* he thought, *compared to back home.*

An image of a gorgeous, building with an ostentatious organ and looming bell tower swam up in his mind. *With Kristina seated at the organ, making the pipes bellow.* Jesse missed his friend. Missed her fiery temper, her fierce loyalty, even her red-gold hair.

Here's another redhead. I seem to find them everywhere. Jesse bit the corner of his mouth to suppress an inappropriate grin.

From the piano bench, a tall, overweight woman in a blue gauzy dress began to sing, "I'll Fly Away." Her voice appealed to Jesse far more than her appearance.

"Who is that?" he breathed into Addie's ear.

"Saloon owner's wife," she replied in an undertone.

How strange.

The song ended and the pastor stood, looking taller than he was, elevated on the stage.

"Let us pray," the little man said in a booming voice that must have emerged from the tips of his toes. "Dear Lord, we gather together today to bid goodbye to our dear Clevis McCoy. This was a man who loved justice, loved his family and loved his friends. He may not have been popular in the eyes of the gossips, but I for one liked him better for his broad-minded views. He leaves behind a beautiful daughter, which is the sort of legacy a man should be proud of. Lord, you promise that those who mourn will be comforted. Comfort us now, and help us remember that in your house, there is no goodbye, only 'see you later'. Because we will see one another again, in your kingdom. Amen."

"Amen," Jesse and Addie echoed.

The two men, along with the undertaker, approached the casket, lifting it onto their shoulders and carrying it out to the churchyard, where a hole awaited. The sight seemed to have a powerful impact on Addie. She staggered and went still, forcing the pallbearers to veer off course to avoid a collision. Carefully they skirted the frozen girl and gently lowered the coffin into the hole.

It hit the bottom with a resounding thud that made Addie jump. A look of agony clouded her features. Quick as he could, Jesse circled the open grave to her and wrapped one arm around her waist. She felt stiff as a church pew and did not in any way melt into his embrace. Knowing there was no way to ease this moment for her, he remained still, supporting her but not trying to stop her from feeling bad. She would feel that way. She had to. Denying it would be worse.

You of all people know how much worse. Addie, being a girl, was allowed to be fragile, allowed to grieve and not put on a strong face. He envied her that. In some way, holding her while she mourned allowed him to lay his own emotions about his friend's passing to rest. Addie could grieve for them both.

Eyes downcast, Addie tossed a handful of dry mountain flowers into the grave. They contrasted sharply with the dark wood of the coffin before disappearing under a shower of earth. She dusted a dirty hand on her skirt and watched with a trembling lip as the undertaker set to work with his shovel.

"Goodbye, Papa," she whispered. "I love you forever."

"He knows that," Jesse reminded her. "He loves you too."

She met his eyes. Her own were a red and swollen mess. "Do you think so, Jesse? Do you think our loved ones remember us in the next world?"

He nodded slowly. "I'm sure they do. What would heaven be without someone to look forward to?"

Addie sniffled.

"Come on, honey. Let's go. You don't need to watch the burial. Your dad is long gone. He's probably corrupting the angels with dirty jokes right now."

A dry, wheezy chuckle emerged, and Addie consented to turn away from the cemetery toward the street. They crossed to the hotel, where a cold supper had been laid out. *I bet Addie won't want food at all, but I'm a bit hungry.*

His hand on her back for support, he led her up the creaking wooden stairs. The front door flung outward, nearly knocking them off the step. A large-bellied man with thinning hair and a ferocious scowl blocked their path. Jesse noted a gold star pinned to the front of his shirt.

"New city ordinance," he boomed. "No half-breeds allowed in public institutions. You can come in, sir, but your whore will have to wait in the street."

What the hell? "Miss McCoy is no whore, and this is her father's funeral. What on earth are you talking about?"

"I'm talking about laws. Do you know about laws, mister?"

"I'm an officer of the law, just like you," Jesse replied.

"Then you'd best take her away. Injuns aren't allowed on these premises."

"Yeah," piped up a belligerent voice from behind the sheriff's shoulder. "Get that filth out of here."

As shock faded to fury, Jesse's fists clenched of their own volition, until Addie closed gentle fingers around his hand. "Let's just go, Jesse. I'm not hungry anyway. Come on."

She led him away down the streets of town for the last time. Her face showed neither regret nor nostalgia for the place she'd lived for who knew how long. Once they'd reclaimed the horse and ridden well away up the side of the mountain, he asked, "What the hell just happened?"

She shrugged. "I can only guess, but it's a good guess. Remember Ed?"

"Yeah," Jesse replied, his eyes on the thin dirt trail that meandered between the pines. It wouldn't do to have Mercury lose his footing on a slippery stone.

"His father owns the hotel, and both of them are close friends with the sheriff. I'm sure this is their revenge for what I did to Ed. His temper would never stand for being taken down by a girl. They already barely tolerated me."

"Sounds like you two had… some history," Jesse commented, steering the horse over a fallen log.

"Yes," she replied but volunteered nothing further.

While the incident still made Jesse's blood boil, in one way he was glad of it. The confrontation had, at least for the moment, distracted Addie from her grief.

"Can you explain," he continued, letting the conversation drift in a different direction, "why you want to stay here? Those folks didn't seem too welcoming, if you know what I mean."

Addie tipped her head back against his shoulder with a sigh. "You're right. They're not. I guess I just… well, I've lost my mother, my father. Everyone I cared about. I didn't want to lose my home. It was a blessing Mr. Miller was willing to buy it. I don't know…"

"Scared?" Jesse asked, keeping his voice gentle and sympathetic.

"A little," she admitted.

"I understand. Throwing over everything you know is scary, but I think you could do better in another place, you know? Maybe your aunt will be wonderful and her town too. Maybe you'll fall in love with someone kind and wealthy and live in a nice house surrounded by friends and family."

Her tense shoulders relaxed a fraction. "That does sound nice, but also like a dream. Remember my mixed blood, Jesse."

"The right man wouldn't care, you know. It only seems unreal because you haven't experienced it yet," he reminded her. "You're young. You're one of the strongest women I've ever met. You'll always rise, Addie."

"I don't feel like I will," she replied, and a shudder ran through her.

"I know. It's hard to see the dawn at midnight. You have to trust that the sun will rise. Believe me, I know suffering and grief. You feel like you want to lie down and die with your loved one. But if you keep on, if you muscle through each agonizing moment, one day you'll wake up and hurt less. You won't feel good, but you'll be in less pain. Another day will be better. Then one day you'll feel happy again."

"You make it seem possible," she said.

"Give yourself time, Addie," he urged. "You'll get through."

"I just feel so alone." Her words caught on a whimper.

"You're not alone," he replied. "I'm here." *Now, where did that come from? You barely know this girl. It would be a stretch even to call her a friend.* But the words could not be unsaid, nor could the inexplicable connection between them be unfelt. Not sure what to do with himself, Jesse concentrated on the rocky majesty of the pine-scented foothills as they ascended to Addie's home.

At last, they arrived at the little house with its ramshackle barn tucked into the shelter of a crag. As they approached, Jesse noted a strange sensation in the air. It felt as though the meadow was holding its breath. The ground beside the stable had been stained red and a strange object lay in a patch of dry, brown grass. As they drew nearer, he saw it was a chicken's head.

Addie slipped from Jesse's lap and ran towards the barn. It stood empty, the cow, mule and all the chickens vanished.

She stood staring when the door to the house opened. Mr. Miller, the man who had purchased the property, stepped onto the porch, a shotgun cradled casually in his hands.

"Y'all move on now," he ordered. "This here is private property."

"But... but..." Addie spluttered.

"You sold it to me fair and square. House, land, barn and all contents. Now git."

Addie shook her head, not as a denial, but as though in shock. "I know," she said, "but I need my suitcase. Mr. Miller, you know my dresses won't fit any of your daughters. Can you just let me get it? You wouldn't send me away with nothing, would you?"

"I don't much care what you do or don't have, half-breed," the man said insolently, "but to show my Christian virtue..." He turned back into the house and a moment later flung a cheap leather case into the yard. The latch burst open, spilling bloomers and stockings across the grass.

"You have one minute before I start shooting," the man sneered.

Addie raced to the case and stuffed all her clothing back inside before running to Mercury. Jesse hauled her onto the horse's back, suitcase and all.

"Now hold on, just a damned minute!" Jesse shouted sliding to the ground. "You bargained with Miss McCoy for her property, but my saddle didn't belong to her to begin with. You steal that, I'll have the law on you. It being in her barn doesn't make it yours."

Miller casually lifted the shotgun in Jesse's direction. "Get it, but you have thirty seconds to get the hell off my property."

"Ride for the tree line, Addie," Jesse instructed. "I'll meet you."

Addie grasped the reins with one hand and nudged Mercury with her heels. Though he danced and fussed at her unfamiliar weight, eventually he obeyed the request.

Meanwhile, Jesse had already entered the barn and grabbed the saddle. Rather than returning to the clearing, where Miller still held the shotgun trained in his direction, he cut around behind the makeshift structure and ducked into the woods, pushing deep enough under the sheltering pines to become invisible. A loud blast sounded, and pellets pinged off the trees, zipping all around him, but none struck home. Jesse circled the property, keeping to the trees, searching for Addie while trying to avoid becoming visible from the house.

A door slammed in the distance, showing that Miller had not intended murder, only a show of insolence, and Jesse relaxed.

Uttering a sharp whistle, he called Mercury to him. The intrepid girl still clung like a limpet to his equine back.

On seeing Jesse, she slid to the ground and threw herself at him. "Oh thank God!" she exclaimed, throwing her arms around his waist. "When I heard that shotgun blast, I thought the worst. Are you all right?"

"I didn't get hit," he replied. "No harm done. And you?"

"He didn't shoot at me," she replied. "I'm fine."

Jesse leaned into the embrace, savoring the warmth of Addie's curvy little body, inhaling the fragrance of her hair. *Like summer flowers and fresh prairie wind.* He touched his lips to the top of her head. She lifted her face to meet his eyes and he couldn't resist the temptation to kiss her warm, smooth forehead as well. Her lips, full and pink, called him like a siren, but he didn't dare. "We should go," he said gruffly, breaking the spell. "I want to put some distance between us and this town before sunset, and we only have a couple of hours"

Addie nodded while Jesse placed the saddle on Mercury's back. *I'm not carrying this damned thing.*

"What should I do with my suitcase?" she asked.

"Do you need the case?" he replied as he tightened the girth with practiced movements.

"Not really. As you saw, it's half-broken already, but what's inside..." she trailed off.

"Yes?" Jesse looked up from his task and saw her holding what looked like a well-worn pair of bloomers. She slowly opened the folded fabric to reveal a glittering metallic pile. "My inheritance, and all the money for the sale of the property. Good thing Miller didn't go through my bag."

"No joke," Jesse replied, eying the double handful of gold and gemstones, and the roll of paper money. "Jewelry?"

"Yes," she concurred. "Dad gave some of it to my mother, which was passed to me. The rest he gave me directly."

Jesse raised one eyebrow. "Help me empty out this saddlebag."

He opened the flap to reveal that the space inside was only partially filled. Working quickly they condensed the contents—some extra ammunition for the pistol that hung in Jesse's belt, two pairs of clean black socks, and a canteen—into the one that contained his own unmentionables and some travel food. Then they stuffed her clothing, with its concealed treasure, in the empty bag.

"You ride," Jesse said. "My legs are longer. We'll make better time that way."

Addie made a face but nodded. Stretching up to stick her boot into the stirrup, she swung herself onto Mercury's back. Though she didn't need the saddle, it clearly didn't bother her to use it.

"Come on," Jesse urged. "Let's get the hell out of here."

Addie gently kicked the horse into motion and the two of them lit out deeper into the sheltering trees, running parallel to the road, but remaining out of sight of it, lest one of the hostile inhabitants decided to cause new trouble.

Chapter 4

They traveled late into the evening. Once clear of the possible range of trouble-makers from town, Addie slipped from Mercury's back and walked, allowing the horse to rest. *What a nightmare. How could things have gone so horribly wrong, so fast?* Addie had never realized just how deep everyone's resentment of her went. They'd tolerated her for her father's sake, but no more, she now knew. It hurt.

"Addie?" Jesse asked, his voice hesitant.

"Hmmm?" She turned to her companion, admiring his firm jaw, his bright blue eyes, his golden hair barely visible under the brim of his black hat.

"What's it like to be…you know… Indian? I've always wondered. I've seen them, and we've never had any trouble, but I don't understand how they think."

Addie shrugged. "I don't exactly know. We lived a very isolated life when my mother was alive, so I think I learned a lot from her, but she died when I was eleven. A year later, we moved to town, or rather near the town. A white woman—the previous pastor's wife—looked after me while my father was away. I learned a lot from her too. It's hard to say what of my feelings and thoughts come from the Kiowa side of me. I've never managed to communicate with any of my mother's relatives."

"Oh," Jesse said, his face curving into lines of disappointment.

"Besides," she continued, "how can anyone explain what they are? It's like asking the water what it is to be wet, or the cloud to be billowy. I think these definitions come more from contrast with others. Without that, it just becomes who you are, what's normal for you. I can say that I have better control of my emotions than some white girls I've known, but not all. I feel a kinship with nature, with the trees and the birds, but my father was much the same way, and his parents emigrated from Scotland just before he was born."

Jesse nodded. She could see he was truly taking in what she said, and she appreciated it. Far too many boys saw girls in general as little more than pretty dolls to set on a shelf and admire. *Like Ed, until he found out…* Shaking off the unpleasant memory, Addie turned her attention to their surroundings again. In order to spare Mercury having to climb all those rocky paths, they had decided to take the long way around, skirting the southern pass of the mountains and approaching Colorado Springs from the southwest, across the prairie.

"Jesse," Addie said a few minutes later, "it's getting dark. Shouldn't we make camp soon?"

"Yeah, I think so," he replied. "I've been trying to find a good place."

She nodded. "What about that clearing up ahead?" she suggested. Before them, the tilted trail leveled out into a small meadow, shaded on three sides by towering Ponderosa pines. The irregular circle of land lacked grass only in a small patch near the center. The burned-out appearance of that patch suggested fires had been set there before.

"I think this will do nicely," Jesse replied. "Can you set up camp? I'll see if there are any rabbits around."

"Sure," Addie replied. They had reached the clearing by this time and Jesse turned Mercury loose to graze. Addie was sure the horse wouldn't wander. He and Jesse were clearly quite close. She wondered if her unexpected champion even realized how unusual he was, to see animals as friends, not to mention girls. *I wonder what makes him so open minded. How many men have I known who see everything as a tool to be exploited? I can't even count that high, but not Jesse. He's like Dad. He understands his place in the world, not as master, but as fellow creature, and works with what he sees.*

Murmuring to the gelding, she removed a roll of blankets from behind the saddle and set them in the grass nearby. The edge of the forest held an abundance of sticks and larger chunks of dry wood. She gathered them quickly and arranged them in the burned-out circle, noting with approval that someone had ringed it with small stones, creating a fire pit.

She retrieved a box of matches from the saddlebag and lit a bed of dried pine needles and leaves underneath the conical arrangement of logs and kindling, and within minutes, a cheerful fire illuminated the growing twilight. Another search of their belongings revealed a small packet of salt. *I hope he finds something good to eat. I'm starving.*

To pass the time, she arranged the blankets into two beds, one on either side of the fire. Both looked a bit thin for the cool of evening. With night, the temperature would surely drop further. She shivered at the thought.

By the time Jesse emerged from the woods, a dead rabbit dangling limply from each hand, full dark had fallen. Worried there would be no dinner, Addie had unearthed some edible tubers—the slender white roots of cattails she'd found at the edge of a nearby pond—which she had tucked into the coals, and a double handful of tough and wizened blueberries. The sight of the plump hares made her mouth water. Carefully setting the berries on a large leaf she'd discovered, where they could wait until breakfast, she drew a knife from her boot and set to work skinning and gutting one of the animals.

"I take it you approve," Jesse joked.

"Of course," she replied. "Good thing you found them. Though squirrel would have worked just as well."

"I have a hard time eating that," he admitted, as he stripped the skin off the second rabbit. "There really aren't any where I grew up, so the taste is… strange to me. I'll eat it in a pinch, but rabbit? We have those everywhere. It's a staple."

She smiled. Jesse could be a bit prissy at times. *Good thing he's handsome to make up for it.* And good thing he could clean a rabbit without a second thought.

Soon the intoxicating aroma of roasting meat wafted through the clearing, making Addie's stomach rumble. To keep her hands busy, she prepared herself for bed, releasing her hair from its pins, brushing it out with her mother's abalone hairbrush, and braiding it up for the night.

She glanced at Jesse, wanting to take off her petticoat, which was an absolute nuisance during the day, and impossible to sleep in. He raised one eyebrow, as though daring her. He made no move to look away. She regarded the woods. Cold and dark. Not a place a girl wanted to be all alone, even for absolute necessities. She had bloomers on.

Meeting his gaze, she fumbled with the ties through the fabric of her skirt and, once they were released, slid the mass of white lace down to her ankles, kicking it away. Though Jesse didn't react one way or the other, she could have sworn his suntanned skin darkened a bit. She smirked, giving herself one point for bravado.

"I imagine tomorrow you're going to wear the divided skirt," he commented, waving a careless hand in the direction of her legs, now clad in unpleasantly clinging black fabric.

"You got that right, pardner," she drawled, affecting a Texas accent. He laughed. "Is that meat about ready?" she asked. "I'm starving."

Jesse lifted one sharpened stick out of the flames and poked at the meat. "A couple more minutes," he replied. "What about those roots?"

Using another stick, one she'd set aside just for this purpose, she poked at her discoveries and found them appropriately mushy. "I wish I had some butter," she complained.

"If milady is unhappy with the accommodations," he replied, pretending to be a starchy waiter, "she can make her way to the luxury car."

"I must say," she joked back, "this train isn't quite what I had in mind." Then, realizing maybe joking wasn't in the best taste, she made a face.

"Addie," Jessie said, "don't worry, honey. Your father would want you to laugh and be happy. He wouldn't want you to waste tears on some tough piece of shoe leather like him." He imitated Clevis's accent perfectly, which drew a smile to her lips… and a tear to her eye.

She drew out her knife again and slit the tubers open, sprinkling salt on their creamy interiors and laying the finally finished rabbit meat on top. The juices sank deliciously into the starch, making a much better meal than they'd expected, given how quickly they'd left town.

They ate in silence. Addie's busy mind finally turned to thoughts of her father, and her loss. Her heart continued bleeding, yet she couldn't help feeling comforted. It was as though everything was as it was supposed to be. As though her father were here, his arm around her shoulders, pointing to Jesse, his friend and protégé, whispering in her ear that here was a reliable, open-minded man who could appreciate her for who she was, not try to fit her into some mold of the perfect woman. *Is this really why you asked him to bring me, Dad? Is there supposed to be something between us? I feel the draw like I haven't in ages, but how can I know?*

And a whisper, like wind in the pines, seemed to answer, "Wait and trust. All will be right in the end. You'll never be alone."

Assured, Addie finished her meal and discarded the bits of gristle and the root peels in the woods, where she went, reluctantly, to tend to her personal needs. Then she returned to her pallet, cleaned her teeth with baking soda, and curled up on the blanket, her arm under her head. As she'd feared, the thin textile neither cushioned her from the rocky ground nor warmed her against the increasingly bitter cold. She squirmed and shivered before drifting into an unsettled sleep.

As she floated between thoughts and dreams, the presence of her father seemed to grow in her mind until she could have sworn he stood in front of her.

"Papa?" she whispered.

"I'm always with you, Addie," the ghostly image replied. "I'll never leave you alone."

"I miss you, Papa," she replied, her voice catching.

"I know, sweetie. I miss you too. I miss hugging you, and talking to you."

"Are you at peace?" she dared ask.

The specter nodded. "It doesn't hurt anymore. I'm safe and fine. You're fine too. Stay close to Jesse. He'll take care of you."

"But who'll take care of him?" she quipped, before realizing the irony of joking with the man she was supposed to be mourning.

She needn't have worried. He threw back his head and roared. "You have him pegged, girly girl. You'll need to take care of him too, but between the two of you, you'll be all right. I can't come back again, Addie. Not like this. You can't see me anymore, but know I'm here. I'll always be right with you."

Addie's giggles abruptly turned to sobs. "Don't go, Papa," she begged. "I need you."

"I can't stay," he replied, his hollow-sounding voice growing increasingly distant. "I love you, Addie. I always have. Be strong. I love you."

"Papa!" she cried. "Papa…"

"Addie, Addie wake up," a low-pitched voice sounded in her ear. She woke with a start to feel Jesse's hand wrapped around her shoulder. The cool night air turned the tears on her face icy and sent drafts of shivery night straight through her. Only where he touched her did she feel warm.

"Jesse!" Addie sat bolt upright and threw herself into his arms.

"Did you have a nightmare?" he asked. "You were crying out in your sleep."

"Not a nightmare," she mumbled in response. "Dad came to me to tell me goodbye." She sobbed.

He cradled her in his arms, rubbing her back. "I know, Addie. I know it hurts. I'm sorry, sweet girl." Again he kissed the top of her head.

"Don't leave me," she begged. "I know it's improper, but I can't stand it. Don't leave me alone."

He didn't protest that his bed on the other side of the fire hardly made her 'alone.' He only rose, grasped his blanket, and carried it back to her. Arranging the one she was using into a pad for the two of them, he lay down beside her and pulled the second blanket over them both. With the front of his body pressed full length against her back, she finally felt warm. Warm and comfortable as though she were lying in a feather bed.

At last, Addie was able to relax.

Chapter 5

Pale pink light filtered through Jesse's closed eyelids, waking him gently. A sense of deep contentment seemed to illuminate his entire being. He opened slowly, taking in the not quite sunrise colors of the sky, pink fading to dark blue, with every imaginable shade of lavender. The wind blowing the evergreen perfume still had a chill bite, but wrapped in his warm wool blankets, his little friend cuddled close to his side, he scarcely felt it.

Ah, Addie. How sweet it is to wake up holding a woman. This must be what it's like to be married. I wonder if any of my friends have taken the plunge. Allie and Wes probably married the first second they could, though I would have expected Kristina to write me about it, and she hasn't said anything. What about Kristina? Did anyone take on her freckles, her music and her German temper? She's a good girl, but it would still be a tall order. I hope whatever she's doing, that she's happy. I hope they're all happy. I do miss them, more than I expected.

A movement in the vicinity of Jesse's shoulder alerted him to the fact that Addie was waking. During the night they'd shifted, him to his back, with her facing him on her side, her head pillowed on his upper chest. Now the clear, soft light of predawn illuminated wide brown eyes that looked deep into him. She seemed to be studying his soul.

"Jesse," she whispered, her full lips bending around his name.

He beckoned with the fingers of his free hand. She scooted up. A strange haze of desire seemed to wash over them both moments before their lips came together. Addie kissed the way she lived, with an utter absence of reticence. Her mouth made free with his, clinging, her hands on his cheeks pinning him in place. Not that he had any desire to move... well, maybe one move. Wrapping his arms around her, he rolled. Now she lay on her back on the ground, and Jesse stretched out above her, his weight braced on one forearm, his free hand shoved into her braid. *This is like coming home.*

He touched her lips with the tip of his tongue, wondering what her reaction would be. Deep kisses normally didn't go over well with a woman, the first time she tried it. Not so Addie. She opened eagerly, tangling her tongue with his.

Okay, so she's done this before. Good. Knowing she wasn't about to go into hysterics, that she understood what he wanted and wanted it too, freed him to explore her with one long, deep kiss after another,

Addie hummed, clearly enjoying their embrace as much as he did. She shifted, unconsciously aligning their bodies. The movement aroused him further, sending blood straight to his groin and engorging his sex. He pumped his hips just a little. Now Addie broke the kiss with a startled squeak.

"Too much?" he asked, smiling at the sight of her blush. "I can't say I'm sorry." He pressed soft kisses to her lips, forehead, nose and back to her lips again.

"Not sorry," she agreed.

"Should we get this day started?" he suggested.

"Yes, I think so," she replied, sounding a bit shy.

He rose and helped her to her feet, groaning as the rigid denim of his jeans compressed his erection.

Addie hurried to the edge of the woods and disappeared into the trees. Jesse shrugged. He wouldn't be able to tend to his personal needs until his engorgement abated a bit, so instead, he added some kindling to the embers of their fire and collected water from the stream to make some coffee in a battered tin kettle he kept at the bottom of one saddlebag.

Soon the girl returned, clad as he'd expected in her divided riding skirt paired with a white pleated shirtwaist, her black funeral garment nowhere to be seen. *Why does it not surprise me she's ignoring the custom of dressing in mourning?* He grinned and left her to make his own trip into the woods.

By the time he returned, two cups of coffee awaited, and the kettle had been pressed into service again, this time for softening hardtack and blueberries in water into a sort of makeshift porridge. Jesse rolled his eyes and drank his coffee. *Not much hope for that sad mush, but at least we'll be able to start off with full bellies. Hopefully, we'll find a town today where we can buy some supplies. I'm low on coffee, and a bit of sugar sure would come in handy. Bet Mercury would like a good meal too.*

A long delay in town would slow their journey, but somehow, Jesse didn't mind.

They'd dawdled over two hours in a little collection of structures too small to be called a town, which sat at the southern edge of the mountain chain they'd just abandoned. At least they'd been able to purchase some food and a hot bath each, plus a bag of hot mash for Mercury. The longsuffering horse seemed much happier to be traversing flat country.

But to pass the night, they chose the open sky once again. This time there was no pretending they would sleep on opposite sides of the fire. They made up their pallet together and lay down, bodies entwined, sending each other into sleep with long, tender kisses.

When morning woke the couple in their nest of blankets, their bodies were already entwined, hands clutching indiscreet parts. Addie had wormed her fingers inside the buttons of Jesse's shirt. His big palm enveloped the swell of her breast. Though she knew what propriety dictated, she made no move to shake him off. His touch pleased her. Already the swollen nipple was responding with tingling satisfaction.

"Mornin', Addie," he murmured in the sweetest sleepy drawl as his hand closed, deliberately turning the accidental touch into a deliberate caress, plucking her nipple and making her moan with pleasure.

"Jesse," she replied, arching her back and pressing her breast closer. He raised one eyebrow at her eagerness. Rather than answer the unasked question in his quizzical expression, she drew his mouth down to hers. *Kissing Jesse is a little taste of heaven. I could go on forever. Just a man, a woman and the open sky. What more could anyone ask?* She led out this time, parting her lips and teasing him with the tip of her tongue.

Mouths deeply mated, Addie guided Jessie's questing fingers to her other breast, which ached for his touch, and he didn't disappoint. Taking a firm grip on the eager bud, he tugged and rolled, making her pant with pleasure. Her thighs parted naturally as moisture surged.

"Nice," he hummed against her lips. "Good enough to eat. What do you say, Addie? Can I take a little taste?"

She bit her lip and opened the buttons of her shirtwaist, baring her chemise to his view. He immediately lowered the front of the garment so her naked breasts experienced the kiss of the sun and the fragrant breeze.

Jesse thumbed one nipple with expert care, and the little brown bud reacted even more eagerly. "I think someone's been naughty," he commented, and then he bent his head, stopping her response with a delicate lap of his tongue. He licked and suckled, drawing moans and sighs of pleasure. One nipple and then the other was subjected to his tender torment.

Addie's toes curled inside her stockings. *Feels so good. Oh, Jesse!* Words escaped her. She could only pant. Heat coiled and spiraled in her belly until her secret places felt swollen and so hot.

"More," she finally managed to gasp. "Please, Jesse. More."

He chuckled and complied, gathering up her skirts to the waist and seeking the open seam of her bloomers.

"Is this what you want, sweet girl?" he asked.

"Ahhhh," she sighed as his questing fingers slipped past the outer lips and delved into her wetness. She wriggled, trying to get his touch to the perfect spot, the little erect nub that seemed to be crying out for him.

He knew. Of course he did, and moved right to it, thumbing her and making her breath catch in her throat.

Jesse was thoroughly enjoying Addie's responses. Clearly, she'd been touched before, maybe by that knucklehead, Ed. That would explain their mutual animosity. At any rate, her willingness delighted him. He'd tried to restrain himself, thinking her a virgin, but he no longer needed to. Now he could enjoy her, they could enjoy each other. Her clitoris swelled hugely under his finger, wet and throbbing. Soon she would reach her peak, and then he could ease into that drenched, clenching passage. *I can't hardly wait.*

But for this, their first time coming together, he would wait, take her slow and easy and be sure she enjoyed it. *If it was Ed, he seemed like he might not know his way around a lady.*

Jesse had plenty of practice in the pleasuring of women, and brought it all to bear on Addie, until she was poised, shuddering, on the precipice of ecstasy. Now she seemed uncertain. *Just as I thought. She's never climaxed before.* Jesse eased her over the edge, teasing gasping wails from her as her body thrashed and clenched. *Soon, soon, soon.* The word repeated like a litany in his mind. Soon he would enjoy the fruits of the labor of passion he was bestowing on this deserving girl.

Still working her bud, he slipped his finger down the cleft of her body and pressed into her passage, gauging her tightness, trying to estimate how slowly he would have to move to keep her comfortable. *Tightest ever.* And then he froze. A thin membrane partially blocked his forward movement.

"Damn it, Addie," he cursed. "You're a virgin!" He pulled his fingers back from caressing her and stood.

She lay sprawled, half-naked on the blanket, her thighs spread wide. She blinked, startled by the rapid transition. "Yes. Did you think I wasn't?"

"Addie, I'm not going to take your virginity!" he exclaimed, shaking his head.

Addie's bare breasts heaved as she hoisted herself into a sitting position. "Explain, Jesse. Why did you think I wasn't a virgin?"

"You were so… eager. You seemed to know how to take a man's touch, you know how to kiss. I just assumed…"

She shook her head, easing her clothing back over her body. "I've kissed and touched a little. Nothing more. But don't forget I also lived on a farm, Jesse. I saw nature in all its rawness. Not to mention, my mother talked to me about the ways of nature. And Dad…he brought home a woman now and again. I have some idea how it works."

"Kissed and touched whom?" Jealous anger flared, and Jesse quickly squashed it down. *What difference does it make, idiot? You can't enjoy her experience and fault her for it at the same time.*

"Ed," she replied with a disgusted sigh, hoisting herself to her feet. "We were engaged last year, so it is a surprise we shared a few liberties? Then he found out… found out I'm half Kiowa. After that, he was done with me. Told me it was no wonder I was such a whore. I don't have to take that from anyone. Needless to say, it ended badly."

"It ended with your boot in his balls and us run out of town at the end of a shotgun," Jesse reminded her.

Addie rolled her eyes.

"Just why were you so eager to give it up to me anyway?" he demanded.

She shrugged, unembarrassed by her behavior. "You're a good man. Good as any. I care for you… and… and I had a dream. Dad seemed to think we'd be good together. I agree. So it seemed like a logical step."

Guilt bloomed in Jesse's gut. *She thought we would be together, that we would be married someday. If I were a different sort of man it might be possible. I could think of a worse woman for a wife.* "I'm sorry, Addie. I didn't mean to lead you on, but I can't marry you or anyone else. I never will. I thought you were the kind of girl who doesn't worry about the rules too much. I wouldn't have minded us... being together during this trip, but that would have been the end of it. Since you aren't that kind of girl... well, your virginity belongs to your future husband. Since that can't be me, I won't take it."

"My virginity belongs to me," she replied, one eyebrow cocked. "I'll give or withhold it as I choose but thank you for clarifying my thinking. I would hate to go on assuming there was a future for us."

"There is a future for us, Addie. As friends. I have always appreciated friendships with women, and I would be honored to consider you one of them."

Addie shrugged—her signature gesture—and plunked down on the ground to pull on her boots.

This is going to be a long day.

Mercury snorted and Addie patted his neck.

Long day indeed, Jesse thought.

Addie had scarcely opened her mouth since they set out from camp. Hour after hour they'd moved forward down a rough, tree-shrouded path, the silence only broken by the soft ring of Mercury's iron shoes on the stones, and the soft sighing of the leather saddle and saddlebags.

He really did feel terrible about the misunderstanding, and now that he'd had a chance to think about it, he could guess how it happened. Addie, being raised by a Kiowa mother, had not been instructed from a young age to hate and fear male attention. He'd heard from many snickering youths that Indian women were 'wanton,' which he took to mean they didn't require marriage to engage in intimacy.

To Jesse's way of thinking, if they were following the rules of their own people, there was no call to judge them for it. He knew they were because he'd seen the results of rule breaking among the various tribes. Harsh punishments were meted out to those who scorned tribal law, torture and mutilation to their enemies.

Growing up with an Indian mother and a mostly absent father must have left Addie with a very different view of intimacy, especially as the cabin in which they lived offered nothing like privacy. She would have been aware of her parents' activities right from the start.

After her mother's death, her caregiver had been a pastor's wife. Jesse doubted the woman had been comfortable talking about such things so she probably hadn't. Adding to that, her father's casual coupling with women reinforced the idea that sex was normal and nothing to be embarrassed about. *She certainly isn't embarrassed.* He'd enjoyed that, her open, responsive embrace. *She'd make a lovely bedmate but she's a virgin, and so I'll never know.*

"Addie," he said, his voice barely audible, "I really am sorry for the misunderstanding. I never meant to lead you on or hurt you."

She smiled without mirth. "It's fine."

They fell back into their uncomfortable silence.

As they rode, Jesse became aware of a darkening sky, a growing cold. *Please don't let it rain.*

His prayer was answered. Instead of rain, fat snowflakes began to drift lazily to earth, caught up occasionally to swirl on the little breezes before settling on the stalks of dry prairie grass and dark, petal-less sunflowers.

Snow in March? How typical. Likely it wouldn't last, at least not at this low elevation, but their ride tomorrow was likely to be wet and uncomfortable. Not to mention camping out tonight. He shook his head. They would have no choice but to share the blankets. He didn't want to freeze.

As he had expected, at bedtime, Addie tried to balk, dragging her covering away from the fire towards the tree line.

"Oh no you don't," Jesse insisted, gripping her arm and escorting her back into their campsite and the warm, roaring fire.

Despite her show of rebellion, she really didn't resist. He had no illusions that she wanted to be close to him after their awkward conversation earlier, but the temperature had dropped from unpleasantly cold to downright icy as twilight deepened, and the lure of the fire and another warm body to share heat couldn't be denied.

She plunked down shivering beside the fire while he fashioned one blanket into a nest. He beckoned, giving her the best spot, with the fire in front of her and his body heat behind. She rolled to face away from him, one arm under her head and flipped the edge of the blanket over herself. He did the same, and then pulled the second blanket, which he'd folded in half, over both of them. If they stayed close, they might just be able to relax.

"Tomorrow night we should be able to sleep indoors. I know of a travelers' cabin. A stove, warm, comfortable beds with quilts, even a bath if anyone wants to heat the water."

"Sounds good," Addie replied, shivering.

"You're stiff as a board," Jesse pointed out, "You'll never be able to sleep like that."

She didn't shrug. Instead, her breath caught on what sounded like a sniffle.

"Don't be sad, Addie," he urged.

"I miss my papa," she replied.

Of course, idiot, Jesse scolded himself. *Don't let your ego get the best of you. She's grieving. Not every sorrow she has is due to you.*

He hugged her a little closer and whispered into her ear, "He'll always be with you. You'll never be alone. Do you believe it, Addie?"

She sagged. "I do."

"Go to sleep. You have a hired gun and a guardian angel watching over you."

"Thank you, Jesse," she said, snuggling back against him.

Addie woke crying in the night again.

As they slept, they'd shifted positions several times, and now her whole front was plastered against Jesse's, her head pillowed on his bicep. Without a word he gathered her close, touching his lips to her forehead, then her cheeks, kissing away her tears. At last, his mouth found hers.

Drowsy and sad, she didn't remember the tense, uncomfortable events of the previous day, but she hadn't forgotten the growing attraction she felt to Jesse. The two of them fit together, heart to heart, mouth to mouth.

He held her as he kissed her, his strong arms encircling her waist. His golden hair felt silky under her fingertips. A thick swelling she understood, though she'd never actually felt one before, compressed against her belly. Thinking only with her heart, Addie surrendered herself to Jesse. Whatever he wanted, she wanted.

This is desire. This is passion. In this moment the world is newly created and me with it. Warmth swelled and spread inside her, touching each secret place with a glow like sunlight through amber. Slow and hot, his tongue penetrated her mouth as he tipped her onto her back and covered her body with his.

"Addie," he murmured, and she could see he was still drowsy, still acting on instinct and not thought.

He rained kisses down her chin and onto her throat, taking a tiny bite at her collarbone and then licking away the sting.

The warmth in Addie's core intensified, spiraling outward to her toes, which curled and flexed inside her stockings. *This isn't love yet, but it could become love.*

Lost in a dizzying swirl of complicated emotions and sensations, Addie didn't protest when Jesse's hand closed over her breast. The pleasure ratcheted up, stopping her breath. The memory of his intimate touch earlier, of the exquisite peak he'd made her feel brought a surge of moisture between her legs. *Only when the two become one is each complete. Only then do both find satisfaction.* Her mother's words echoed in her heart. *That's what I crave. Oneness with Jesse. He completes me, and I complete him. Surely he must feel it too.*

So when his fingers delved under her skirt, she allowed the touch. His cold fingers shocked her molten core, and the touch seemed to startle him as much as it did her.

"Addie..." He seemed suddenly awake and startled. "Addie, I'm sorry, I..." His hand pulled back.

"Don't stop!" she begged, urging his fingers back into her secret depths. "Touch me."

"Addie, I can't. I'm sorry, you know I won't take your virginity."

"Then don't," she urged. "Only please don't stop. I'm burning, Jesse."

Burning, sweet girl? You don't know the half of it. The things I can do to make this sweet flesh hot. A wicked voice seemed to whisper in his ear, *If you don't finish the act, you can touch her all she wants. Her future husband will never know. You'll be her delicious secret for the rest of her life. Her lover who didn't dishonor her.*

He pressed one finger into her and examined her hymen. The membrane seemed sturdy enough not to rupture easily. *Too bad for her, but good for me.* He slipped past its opening and deep into her body.

"Ahhhhh," Addie sighed. "That's good, Jesse." Her voice sounded thick like sun-warmed honey. He didn't dare thrust his finger inside her, so he rotated his hand, palm up, and found a special spot at her fullest depth, which he tickled with expert precision, simultaneously caressing her clitoris with his thumb.

Her knees locked, her body tensed. She seemed to be reaching for what he wanted to bring her.

Gasps and cries echoed off the pine trees as Addie reached her climax, and Jesse imagined what that tight, innocent passage would feel like gripping his erection. His own arousal had grown painful while he tended to his lady's needs. *Patience. Patience, Jesse. Let her have her moment.*

At last, Addie lay limp and panting, and Jesse withdrew his fingers from her intimate flesh. "My turn," he told her, taking her hand and guiding it inside his trousers. He curled her fingers around his tumescence and showed her how to stroke him. A few slow, easy movements had him on the brink. Rising quickly from their bed, he stepped away and deposited his seed on the cold ground.

Shivering, he returned to their nest of decadent love play, slipping his arms around Addie again. She snuggled up against him, finally comfortable. With their passion sated, they slipped easily into a peaceful sleep.

While she slept a different sensation of warmth and a comforting presence swirled around Addie.

"Who's there?" she called into the darkness.

There was no answer, but none was needed. No matter how the years passed, certain sights, sounds and scents would always remain potent in her memory.

"Mama?" Addie asked.

"Of course, little one," came the reply.

"Why are you here, Mama?" she asked.

"I've come to collect your father," she replied, her normally serene voice sparkling with amusement. "He seems to have lost his way, but I will always find him. We were meant for each other, you know."

"Yes," Addie replied. "I'm sure of that."

"But while I was here, I wanted to check up on you."

"Oh!" Addie felt a flash of embarrassment, even though she knew she was dreaming. "Did you see...?"

"I saw. You've found your soul mate. He's a good man, but a stubborn one with many silly ideas. You will have to be more stubborn than he is."

Addie cast her dreaming eyes downward in the direction of her feet. They looked real, for all they weren't standing on anything that appeared to be solid. "He says he can't be with me."

"He can. He only thinks he can't. He doesn't realize that the heart does not break once for all time. He doesn't know how much he's healed. How ready he is for a new chapter to unfold. Be strong and patient. You are the water. He is the rock. Water can shape rock, but you will need to use slow pressure and time. Pressure and time, Adeline."

"I don't know if he's really worth so much. Sometimes I don't think much of him," Addie admitted. "I mean, he's attractive, but he's also…"

"Fearful. Do not let yourself believe that fear is all he has. He fears loss and suffering. He fears losing more of himself, but he's braver than most in other ways. You can heal his fear and he can heal yours. The two of you complement each other, but his mind and heart are not ready, could not be made ready without you. This is your test as well as his, daughter. Who is more stubborn? Only you can decide that. He will yield if you do not give up."

Addie sighed. "I wish you were here, Mama. Dad too. It's hard being alone."

"You are not alone, Adeline. You have never been alone. Remember that."

"Yes, Mama."

"I must leave you now. Remember my words. Tenacity, strength and time. You will earn your heart's desire."

And then Addie found herself alone in her own mind, as pink light filtered through her closed eyelids revealing that dawn had arrived. She woke slowly, enjoying the warmth of the light, and the even greater warmth of the man who held her close in his arms. *Tenacity, strength and time will wear away his fears.*

Good advice, if she had the courage to take it. *He could just as easily break my heart.*

Chapter 6

The journey toward Colorado Springs passed in days of conversation and nights of naughty caressing. Try though he might, Jesse could feel no guilt about laying his hands all over Addie's sweet body. She, in turn, proved to be a most comfortable and relaxing bedmate, demanding only the pleasure he enjoyed giving her, and once she learned how, returning the favor eagerly.

When they weren't playing on the safe edges of passion, they were able to talk about a number of subjects. She rarely expressed interest in the girly things that normally bored him, like clothing, but she had sensible, informed opinions on various makes of guns, a vast wealth of knowledge about edible and medicinal plants, and an interest in history, one of his favorite subjects. Easy conversation made the long days pass swiftly.

Jesse felt tremendously relieved that Addie's sulk hadn't lasted long. They were fast becoming good friends... the best kind of friends. He couldn't keep a satisfied smirk off his face. He turned away to conceal it from her, but to no avail.

"What are you smiling about?" she demanded in mock outrage.

"How good you taste," he replied, unabashedly watching her cheeks turn pink at the memory of his mouth on her lower parts. That had strained even her considerable aplomb. At the time, of course, she squirmed and shuddered like the hot-blooded wench she was, but in the cold light of day, her blushes charmed him as much as her uninhibited response had the previous night.

"You're evil," she muttered.

"And that's just the way you like me," he retorted with a grin.

"You're right," she admitted, meeting his eyes and smiling. "So where do we stop tonight? Are we camping again?"

Jesse shook his head. "There's a town a little ways down the road. I have friends there. One owns a boarding house. She'd be terribly offended if I didn't stay with her while I was in town."

"How will you explain me?" Addie asked.

"As a friend in need of an escort," he replied mildly. "It's true, after all. Don't worry, Addie. I may be a bounty hunter, but I have a good reputation. I don't think anyone will assume the worst."

Addie gave him a look that clearly told him he was crazy but didn't answer.

A couple of hours later, the town loomed up ahead of them. Unlike the low collections of plank and brick structures they'd passed so far, Cañon City, Colorado, was a proper town, with three and four-story structures looming over a wide cobblestone street. As they proceeded, Addie noted a red-brick hotel, three stories high and trimmed in green, the words St. Cloud Hotel emblazoned across the front. Several stately homes of the painted lady variety stood along the street, their opulence interspersed with mundane businesses and tumble-down shacks. From one, the rank stink of untended outhouse fouled the air.

"Doesn't this town have a sewer?" Addie asked, holding her nose.

"Of course," Jesse replied, "but not every house has elected to connect to it."

Addie shuddered, and then changed the subject. "Since we passed the hotel, I assume we're staying elsewhere? You mentioned a boarding house?"

"That's right," Jesse replied. "A friend of mine, Mrs. Phillips, owns it. Her husband built it for her in anticipation of having many children, but they only had one daughter. Then he died in a stagecoach robbery. I brought in the robber, and he was hanged. Mrs. Phillips has absolutely insisted I stay at her boarding house whenever I'm in town. She never lets me pay either." A hint of a smile crossed Jesse's face, making Addie wonder if he'd comforted the widow in ways other than bringing the killer to justice.

Not liking the jealous feelings these unsubstantiated thoughts raised in her, she returned to her survey of Main Street. Behind the first row of structures, a second street at a higher elevation sported a church with a towering steeple and several more homes. Behind that, the backdrop of the grassy hill cut off abruptly into a blue, sunny sky.

"It's pretty here," she commented.

"Yes," Jesse replied. "It reminds me of home, in spite of the hills."

"Where's home?" she asked him.

"Garden City, Kansas," he replied. "Small and remote, and terribly, terribly flat."

"Do you miss it?"

He shrugged. "Maybe, but I don't miss the memories."

I wonder what unspoken agony just twisted his face so harshly. Something terrible must have happened there. Poor Jesse.

"I know what you mean," Addie said in her gentlest voice. She reached down from Mercury's back and squeezed his shoulder. He rested his hand on hers briefly before they continued on their way.

"Here we are," Jesse exclaimed, indicating a three-story painted lady in a soft gray tone with masses of gingerbread hanging from the eaves.

Addie nodded approvingly at the subtle color. *Like a winter sky, not garish the way some of these are painted.* The house seemed to blend into the landscape as though it had grown up from the earth.

A hitching post at the front gate identified the building as a business rather than a residence. Jesse lifted Addie down from Mercury's back and tied up the horse before escorting her up onto the broad, welcoming white porch. A knock at the door was quickly answered by a woman who appeared to be about thirty years of age, her glossy brown hair pulled back into a braided bun, her generous curves hugged by a dress the same color as her house. She smiled a broad, gap-toothed smile and threw her arms around Jesse.

"Jesse, darling!" she gushed, squeezing him until his ribs creaked. Addie ground her teeth.

"Good to see you too, Anne," he replied in a rasping wheeze. "Don't break my ribs."

"Sorry!" The brunette released him with a kiss on the cheek. A pink stain remained behind.

Hmmm, Addie thought. *I wonder if the curves are as false as the lips.*

"Anne, this is my friend, Adeline McCoy. She recently lost her father, and I'm bringing her to her aunt in Colorado Springs."

"Pleased to meet you, Miss McCoy," the bubbly widow replied, her tone significantly restrained compared to how she'd greeted Jesse. "I'm sorry to hear about your loss."

"Thank you," Addie replied in a cool, soft voice.

"Jesse, your usual room is available," the woman said, turning her back on them. "Miss McCoy, if you'll follow me, I'll show you to yours. I have men and women on different floors, for propriety's sake. Women are on the third floor... and the stairs creak like a shotgun. It protects everyone's reputation, you know. Breakfast is served at eight, lunch at noon, and dinner at seven. Let me know if you plan to eat, so I can have enough food."

"We'll have dinner tonight, for sure," Jesse said. "And likely breakfast too, but we're only staying tonight. This young lady is expected in Colorado Springs, and I'd like to see her safely there."

"Be careful out there," the woman replied. "There's a lot of unrest going on. A gang of train robbers has been troubling the high plains from Dodge City to Liberal. Rumor says they might have a hideout somewhere in the mountains."

Jesse froze. "Train robbers on the High Plains? Has Garden had any trouble?"

"I haven't heard," the woman replied. "But who knows? Garden is so small, it's easy to overlook."

Jesse stepped back outside, apparently to collect their belongings and tend to Mercury while Mrs. Phillips led Addie up two flights of stairs; mahogany wood with polished banisters and a studded black runner up the center.

As predicted, the second staircase protested loudly under their combined weight. If anyone tried to sneak up during the night, they'd be caught instantly. *Looks like I'll have to behave for one night anyway.* It shocked Addie how desolate the thought made her. *Falling in love in two weeks is stupid. I'm not stupid. It isn't love.*

She had to face the fact that she had a silly schoolgirl crush on Jesse West. *It's not his fault. He told you he can't love you. All he can do is play with you a while, and you agreed to it. Hell, Addie, you begged for it. If you get your heart broken, it's your own fault.*

For a moment the two dreams of her parents floated up before her, but she pushed them away. *Dead parents don't come back in dreams to advise the living.* She was on her own now, an adult, and her first adult decision had been decidedly unwise.

And yet, before you part ways from Jesse for good, you will let him touch you again. There was no denying it.

Mrs. Phillips led her through a long hallway with gas lights mounted on the walls and a smooth ceiling with plaster medallions every few feet, past several doorways to the very end, where she unlocked the last door on the right and handed Addie the key.

"Water closet is across the hall. See you at dinnertime," the woman said curtly and walked away without a word.

Addie stepped over the threshold into a smallish room with a single bed, attractively framed in brass bars and warmed by a thick, blue and green crazy quilt. A bureau hugged the far wall, and a window on either side of the bed emitted spring sunlight in rectangular patches on shiny wood floorboards and a small green rag rug.

A series of loud creaks indicated someone coming up the stairs, and a moment later, Addie was unsurprised when a heavy hand knocked on her bedroom door.

She opened to find Jesse extending a bundle towards her. "I wrapped all your things in one of the blankets," he said by way of explanation.

She took the bundle and set it on the bed, returning to her friend and regarding him with shy eyes. *Ironic how we can lie together with our hands all over each other outside, but a bedroom makes me feel timid.*

"Nice room," he said, clearing his throat.

"Thanks," she replied.

"Well, I'd better go."

"Yeah, see you at dinner?"

"Sure."

With that deadpan exchange, Jesse turned to leave. Addie began to close the door.

"Oh wait…" Jesse stepped back in her direction.

"Did you need something?" Addie asked.

"Yes," he replied, grabbing her chin and pressing a quick kiss to her lips.

Then, like a naughty schoolboy, he fled down the hallway and disappeared down the stairs.

Feeling like a moonstruck girl, Addie touched her fingertips to her lips. Then she slowly shut the door and moved to the bed where she unwrapped her bundle and considered whether she had time to wash any of her clothes.

Jesse's heart pounded a long time after he left Addie standing stunned in the door of her bedroom. *I've kissed her dozens of times. Why was that one so different?* It must be the bedroom. In nature, it was easy to do what was natural. Houses and bedrooms changed things. Imposed rules. A boy could kiss his sweetheart at the door, but he'd best not cross the threshold.

She's not your sweetheart, you ass. Being in town suddenly made Jesse feel like a cad. He knew—could see—that Addie had not abandoned the idea that they might have a future. *Soon she'll be feeling a bit abandoned.* He winced. *Maybe...* he shook his head.

There was no way he could keep her. Not as the girl he visited when he passed through her town and felt lonely. That would be a grave disservice to her. Nor could he marry her, for the same reason. While she sat home and worried, he'd be out chasing bail jumpers and bank robbers. He might never come home, and she might never know why. *Not to mention she deserves a husband who can adore her.*

Steeling his heart once again against the potent lure of her big brown eyes, he stalked out into the yard to tend to his horse.

Chapter 7

That night, dinner consisted of some of the best fried chicken Addie had ever eaten. The skin had been breaded in a flavorful crust and had the scorch marks consistent with a cast-iron skillet. The meat dripped savory juices with every bite. As a veteran of many failed attempts to fry chicken, Addie's respect for the flamboyant brunette rose a few degrees. As did the appearance of her daughter at the table. The child, who looked to be somewhat under ten, showed no fear conversing with all the adults at the table and regaled them with funny stories about the children at school.

As dessert—a meltingly tender apple crisp—arrived on the table, the girl fell silent, intent on shoveling seasoned apples and crunchy oats into her mouth. One of the men spoke up.

"So, West, you just passing through?"

"That's right," Jesse replied.

"You oughta come back this way," the man urged, wiping a drip of spiced and thickened juice from his thick, bulbous lip. "There's some trouble 'round these parts. Don't rightly know what it is, but a few homesteads have been robbed, some burned, and I think there may have been a murder, way out on one of the remote farms. Leastaways, they found two bodies burned in their beds. It had been too long to tell if anything else had happened."

"That's enough of that, Mr. Jones," Mrs. Phillips snapped with a sidelong glance at her daughter.

"Sorry, ma'am," he replied sheepishly, taking another bite of his dessert.

"I might stop by," Jesse offered. "Is there any reward money available?"

"Not exactly," Mrs. Phillips admitted. "But if it's an organized gang, you can bet someone's on a wanted list somewhere."

"All right," Jesse said, a bit coolly. *He doesn't seem too keen on that idea,* Addie thought. Then her first bite of apple crisp drove every thought right out of her head.

Despite the comfortable feather mattress on which he lay, and despite the fat pillow under his head, Jesse couldn't sleep. The heavy pile of quilts on his bed seemed to smother him. The embers in the fireplace glowed too brightly. It was as though he'd become accustomed to sleeping outside, with the fresh air and the sky above. *And a sweet brown-eyed girl in your arms.*

He shoved the thought away. In two days they would arrive at their destination and he would deliver Adeline to her aunt. He doubted he'd ever see her again. The thought didn't sit well. In fact, it nagged at him. *If you care for her, you'll do what's best for her,* his annoying, long-ignored conscience insisted. *What's best for her is a future with a husband who hasn't had his heart broken, who can lavish on her all the love and attention she deserves. She's special, and she deserves to be treated like she is.*

He knew it was true, so why did it feel like weasels were chewing on him, in the hollow where his heart used to be? Shaking off the sad feelings, he rolled over and willed himself to go to sleep.

"I won't miss that town," Addie commented, glancing over her shoulder at the horizon, where Cañon City remained barely visible.

"What's wrong with it," Jesse asked.

Addie lifted her shoulders in her signature shrug. "I think there were a lot of gossips there. And that boarding house woman? She's in love with you."

"Naw." He dismissed the comment with a wave of his hand. "It was never love. She wanted someone to talk to…"

"And something more, right, Jesse?" Addie demanded.

He felt his cheeks growing hot despite the cold of the day. "Yeah," he admitted. "But only a couple of times. She couldn't accept it was just for fun, and got… possessive, so I had to break things off. I'm not sure she ever accepted it."

The similarity between that situation and this dawned on him, bringing a wave of embarrassment. *You have a bad habit of doing this, Jesse West. Didn't you learn from Anne that decent, vulnerable women don't want casual sex?* Apparently, he hadn't learned, and now another good woman was about to be hurt by his carelessness.

Jesse took hold of Addie's calf, where it rested above the stirrup. He didn't speak, but tried with all his might to send... something... he didn't even know what, directly to her.

Her eyes remained on the horizon. "How long will it take to get to our destination?" she asked.

"To our campsite tonight? Most of the day, naturally. We should arrive in Colorado Springs tomorrow afternoon."

She nodded and fell silent again. The discomfort he thought they'd gotten past ages ago had come back with a vengeance.

Night had fallen long before Jesse and Addie settled for the last night in their blankets. This time they'd chosen a small meadow, surrounded by trees, on the side of a tall hill. To either side, the forest concealed a narrow road. Behind them, a sheer, rocky surface seemed more mountain than foothill. Before them, the embankment fell away sharply, revealing a long, steep drop to the icy river below. He expected her to lie rigid against him, sharing body heat but nothing more.

He couldn't have been more wrong. No sooner did they settle in than she rolled over to face him, drawing his head down to press ravenous kisses to his mouth.

"Addie?"

Her only response was to slip her fingers inside his shirt and caress his chest.

"Addie, I don't think we should do this, honey."

At last, he had captured her attention. "Why not?"

"I don't want you to get hurt."

She met his eyes, and the warm brown had turned to a whiskey color in the firelight. *Deep and rich enough to drown in, and worth every moment.*

"It's too late. You can't stop me from getting hurt now. I care too much for you. So since you can't stop my heart from bleeding, at least give me something to remember, Jesse. One last night."

The wounded innocence in her eyes proved to be his undoing. He lifted her chin and pressed his lips to hers in a kiss of aching tenderness and regret. *I wish I could be different. Addie is worth it.* The ache in his chest remained, unabated, and so he knew he still couldn't be all Addie needed and desired.

But I will give her a night to remember, a night to satisfy her dreams until she meets that special man. The thought of another man touching Addie made him want to grit his teeth and hit something, but instead, he soothed his unwarranted jealousy by focusing his attention on pleasuring his girl one last time. As he ravaged her mouth with long, wet kisses as he skimmed his hands up her torso to cup the generous fullness of her breasts. *Nice, and surprisingly big for her small stature.*

Addie helped him access her by opening the buttons on her blouse. He wasted no time lifting one plump breast free and seizing the nipple with ravenous eagerness. Addie's hands laced into his hair and she held him pinned in place, insisting he tend the sensitive bud to her satisfaction, and then she guided him to the other side.

Far from wanting to protest, Jesse gladly sucked and nibbled the pebbled peaks, enjoying the naughty taste of her.

She unbuttoned his shirt as well, sliding her hands along the solid muscles of his chest. He hummed at the sweetness of her touch, her strong, calloused fingers making him shiver. Without hesitation, she unbuckled his belt and then opened the fastenings of his jeans, worming her hand into the tight denim to grasp his rigid length.

Jesse groaned at the touch. *I'd love to be touched by this woman every day of my life.*

Shoving away the thought, and also his clothing, he turned to Addie and slowly stripped away her skirt, chemise and bloomers. Her breath caught in her throat.

"Open, Addie," he urged, pressing outward on her thighs. She parted for him. He kissed his way down her torso until he could part the lips of her sex and run his tongue along the salty-sweet folds between.

Addie released a whimpering cry at the intimate touch and moisture surged against his tongue. He lapped and nibbled at the lacy folds and in the meanwhile inserted one finger deep into her, always careful not to damage the proof of her innocence.

Addie tilted her head back and let out a soft cry. *She's so responsive. What a woman.* Jesse focused his attention on Addie's pleasure, working her love button with his lips and tongue, tickling deep inside her with one fingertip. He watched her as her pleasure built and built within her, watched her climb recklessly towards the summit of ecstasy. He took great pleasure in knowing that it was his touch, his skill, making her feel so good. With a whimper she tumbled into the abyss, her muscles locking, her passage clamping down on his finger. *I can just imagine what that would feel like, all tight and clinging.* She made a soft sound of protest as he withdrew from her, aligning his sex with hers.

Her eyes flew open. "Jesse?"

"Trust me, Addie." He thrust his hips, not to enter her, but to slide his erection along her wet, heated flesh, stimulating himself and her in one movement.

"Ahhhh," she sighed.

"That's it, sweet girl, enjoy it," he urged. He knew he would. The heat of her perfect female flesh enveloped him. *Careful, careful, Jesse. Not too fast, not too hard. Enjoy this last taste of Addie.*

His seed was rising, and he couldn't stand against it. At last, with a groan, he slid along the entire length of her wetness and erupted, splattering her with hot, viscous liquid.

"You know something, Jesse?" she asked in a breathless voice.

"What's that?" he wheezed.

"You're too much a gentleman for your own good."

He chuckled, kissed her lips and sponged the semen from her belly and mons with a dirty piece of clothing. "Sleep well, Addie."

She cuddled up against him and closed her eyes. He kissed her cheek and found it wet, but refrained from commenting on her tears.

Addie sat by the embers of the faltering fire. Jesse had retired to the woods around the corner for a bit of privacy. Soon they'd be off for the last day of their journey. *The last day Jesse will be in my life.* She could still feel the wetness of his seed on her inner thighs from where they'd played again, just as dawn pierced the horizon.

The last time. She wiped tears away from her cheeks. *I told him how I have better control than most girls. I boasted about it. Look at me now, sniveling like a little baby.*

Her harsh thoughts did nothing to assuage her grief.

Off in the woods, a twig snapped. Her eyes immediately darted that direction, but she could see nothing. *Probably a deer.* There were mountain lions too, in these woods, and they sometimes attacked travelers. Mercury also raised his head up from the dry grass he'd been nibbling, a disgusted expression on his equine face, his warm dark eyes scanning the tree line.

"What is it, boy?" she asked the horse. Mercury whickered in response. "Jesse," she called. "Is that you?"

Something sharp and icy touched Addie's throat. She gasped and a little yelp escaped. Mercury echoed the cry with a loud whinny.

A heavy, tobacco-smelling hand clamped over her mouth. "Stand up, girly, nice and slow," a raspy voice growled in her ear.

When the man exerted upward pressure, she acquiesced, terrified she might be cut. Her heart pounded in her ears and she felt a strong urge to gag.

"Where is he?" the man snarled. "Where's the bounty hunter?"

He loosened his hold on Addie's mouth, but the knife against her throat didn't waver.

"I don't know," she said honestly.

"You're going to take me to him, help me catch him. We can't have bounty hunters hanging around these parts."

"He's here to take me to my aunt's house," Addie protested. "He's not here for you."

"We can't take chances. Help me find him, girly, help me catch him, and you'll live to see your aunty."

Addie squeezed her eyes shut. The lascivious drawl in his voice told her what would happen before her alleged release. *Damn you, Jesse, did you preserve my virginity for a gang of rapists?*

But this was not a gang, at least not yet. If only something could distract him, she could form a plan.

"What the hell?" Jesse's exclamation burst through the clearing, sending birds into the air with startled squawks. A squirrel scolded from the top of a nearby pine. "Get your filthy hands off my girl!"

"Not so fast, partner," the man replied in a phony casual tone. "I'll turn loose of your girl… eventually, but not before I have a little taste. She looks downright tempting."

"Bastard!" Jesse took a threatening step forward.

"Careful," the man replied. "One little slip…" he jiggled the knife and nicked Addie's skin. Warm blood ran down her neck.

Jesse froze. Addie whimpered and made a movement with her hands as though seeking support by grabbing the villain's clothing.

Just as I suspected. A desperate plan took shape in Addie's mind. She met Jesse's eyes, schooling her face to calmness, and deliberately closed one eye, not in a wink, but to catch his attention.

Jesse did not react to her gesture in the slightest, but she could only hope he'd gotten her message.

"She's not really worth all this fuss, man."

"Ha, that's not what I saw this morning," the villain scoffed, clutching one of Addie's breasts.

Jesse shrugged. "She's a decent bit of skirt, nothing more. You don't really think you can get me to sacrifice myself for the sake of a half-breed slut, do you?"

Addie took a deep breath. It hurt to hear Jesse saying these things, even though she knew he didn't mean them.

Casually, Jesse removed his gun from its holster. "You'll never draw in time to live."

"I'll take her with me." The knife bit deeper.

Jesse lifted one shoulder. "You'll be dead either way. Tell me, man, how much is your carcass worth?"

The tension in the man's body shifted. His attention was now focused on Jesse and not on her. *I might not survive this, but I have to try.*

In one fluid movement, she reached behind her, grabbed the gun she'd found strapped to his hip and turned it backwards, shooting him in the thigh and at the same time twisting in the direction of his entrapping arm, crowding close to his body to escape the knife. She sat straight downward as a second pistol roared. Something flew over her head as she ducked, snipping a chunk out of her hair.

The bandit yelled as he staggered backwards. The knife dropped from his hand and sank deep into the ground, pinning the corner of Addie's divided riding skirt and only missing her leg by an inch.

She whipped her head around to see the villain who had grabbed her—a grizzled man with sagging jowls like aged leather—clutching his shoulder. Everything had happened so fast, he was still stumbling backward with the impact of Jesse's bullet on his shoulder when Addie turned. The man's last step connected with a slick stone and his feet went out from under him, sending him tumbling. His legs landed on the rocky ground, but his head, torso and hips didn't, and he fell over the steep embankment headfirst, screaming until his cry ended in a sickening crunch.

Silence descended on the impromptu campsite, broken only by the sound of blood rushing in Addie's ears and a strange ringing which must have been a result of the pistol's loud report. She concentrated on drawing air into her lungs, ignoring the messy cut still dripping tickling droplets onto her bosom.

"Addie?" She started violently at the sound of Jesse's voice. "Are you all right?"

She nodded slowly.

"You're bleeding!"

She raised trembling fingers to her throat and was stunned to see them come away stained red. At last her eyes focused on the scene. A lock of burnished hair lay on a gray rock beside her, snipped from her head by a bullet. The knife that had cut her was now stuck through her skirt. A pistol slipped from her sweat-slickened hand and tumbled to the ground, a wisp of smoke still rising from the muzzle.

Jesse's face appeared in front of hers without warning. She screamed and scrambled back a bit, slitting the hem of her skirt as it escaped the bite of the blade.

"Addie, it's me. You sure you're okay?"

Her vision blurred.

In a heartbeat, Jesse had plunked himself down on the ground and hauled her into his lap, where he slowly rocked her back and forth, murmuring as though to a frightened child.

Addie nestled into his warmth. She felt cold and disoriented, not quite sure what had happened. All she knew in that moment was that this—these warm arms, this familiar scent—represented safety. She never wanted to leave the cradle of his embrace.

"What happened?" she asked.

"A man attacked our camp. Attacked you. You shot him with his own gun. My brave, strong girl." He crushed her in his arms. "I thought he was going to kill you. I thought I was going to watch you die. Oh God, Addie."

He kissed her lips.

She liked the warmth of his embrace, so she kissed him back, and then again, and again. Without warning the kiss exploded into a fiery passion Addie could never remember having experienced before. Even while they played at lovemaking, she'd never felt anything like this. Gripping two handfuls of Jesse's shirt, she pinned him in place so she could devour his mouth with hers. He crushed her in his arms.

The world tilted around her and the next thing Addie knew, she lay on the ground, Jesse's solid weight pinning her down. Frantically he delved under her skirt. Her bloomers still lay on the ground a ways off, and Jesse took advantage of her nakedness to slip two fingers past the coarse auburn hair between her thighs and push deep into her body. Her wetness from all their love play the previous night and this morning allowed the rough penetration.

"Uhhh," she moaned, more in pain than pleasure. She'd taken one finger well enough, but two stretched her uncomfortably. *You're about to discover what more than just two fingers feels like,* she realized, noticing Jesse was yanking at his belt.

She uttered not one word of protest, instead hiking her own skirts up to bare herself to him.

Jesse shoved his jeans to his knees and covered her body with his.

Addie laced her fingers through the back of his hair and pulled him down, wanting nothing more than to drown her senses in more of his delicious kisses. With her free hand, she reached down low and took hold of his jutting erection. Acting on pure instinct, she guided it to the entrance of her body.

No sooner had their bodies aligned than Jesse shoved hard, pinning her body to the ground with the force of that first thrust.

"Owwww," Addie whimpered. There was no gentleness, no tenderness to Jesse's taking. While she understood why, understood his terror over their near disaster, the hard, rough way he was moving in her just plain hurt.

"I'm sorry, Addie," he panted. "I know it stings but I," he gasped. "Can't." Another sharp inhalation. "Stop."

And he didn't stop. He rode her hard and deep, slamming into her virgin passage with the force of a rampaging stallion and battering the mouth of her womb.

Addie squirmed against the onslaught. Jesse slid his hands under her buttocks and lifted her to the angle he desired. The shift in position brought with it a change in sensation. Now the end of his penis was scraping and nudging that special spot he'd found inside her. Heat tingled, mingling with the soreness. Then it grew, spreading and radiating out from her stinging passage into every inch of her body. Though she would never have thought it possible, the discomfort of her rough deflowering was rapidly changing into something different. Tension thrummed, taut as a bowstring, in every nerve.

A delicate whimper escaped, then another, and then a full-throated scream as pleasure obliterated pain in a soul-deep orgasm.

The sound of Addie's scream wrested Jesse from his haze. *Dear God, what am I doing?* Exactly what he'd promised not to do. Taking her virginity. *Took. It's done. You've claimed her.* Concerned, he looked down into her face and saw to his astonishment that she was climaxing. The clamping of her sex proved it. Wetness surged, easing his way to greater penetration until at last he could take no more and released his own pleasure into her waiting depths.

He lay gasping on top of Addie's body, his mind blank, all wildness burned away by their mutual passion.

She didn't speak, only stroked his back. Clutched in the most intimate of embraces, they dozed.

When Jesse opened his eyes, he found Addie still sleeping. Her face relaxed, but the nick on her throat still livid. He touched his lips to the spot. His stomach clenched again as he thought of how close he'd come to losing her for good.

And now you've claimed her for good. He acknowledged the fact and considered what to do about it. *I always said her virginity should belong to her husband. Should I marry her? Being married to Addie wouldn't be bad.*

Wouldn't be bad… for him, but what about her? She'd be stuck for the rest of her life with a man who had no heart, a man no longer capable of love.

But she's no longer innocent, his outraged conscience argued… at least, that where he assumed the little voice was coming from.

He firmed his resolve. The right man would overlook such a thing, not worry about one mistake, any more than he'd worry about her Kiowa blood. *It's more important than ever to stick to your convictions. Stay the course, man. She isn't for you, and this changes nothing.*

Chapter 8

"I can't believe this," Addie sobbed, staring down the road through tear-veiled eyes at a small house tucked into a little valley about a mile south of Colorado Springs. The town remained visible, as the property had a bit of elevation, but the snug little cabin still had plenty of elbow room.

"What do you mean? I've told you all along this was how it would be, Addie. I've never lied to you."

"You also promised you wouldn't take things so far."

Jesse's pale cheeks colored. "I didn't mean to do that. I lost control. I'm really..."

"Don't you *dare* say you're sorry, Jesse West. Don't you dare," Addie hissed. "I will *not* be one of your regrets."

Jesse stopped his forward motion and turned towards Addie. They were both on foot at this point, Mercury ambling along beside them. "Nevertheless I am sorry. I shouldn't have done what I did, and I'm sorry you're hurting, Addie, but nothing has changed. The reasons I couldn't be with you are the same."

"And what would those be?" she demanded, planting her fists on her hips. "I think you owe me that much anyway."

"Well, for one thing, my life is dangerous. I wouldn't be able to keep you with me. I'd be worrying about you all the time, and that would put me in danger. I'd have to have you stay somewhere I knew you'd be safe, and I don't think a place like that exists. Even if it did, you'd be there, alone, for weeks or even months on end, never knowing if I was alive or dead."

"What if I decided that was acceptable?"

Jesse reached out one big, calloused hand and cupped her cheek. Despite her rage, Addie couldn't help but lean into his touch. "You shouldn't accept that. You deserve better, Addie. Have you ever been in love, honey?"

She met his eyes and saw a deep, deep pain looking back at her. "Yes."

He nodded. "I was, once. Heart and soul, nothing held back."

That's how I feel about you, you idiot. "What happened?"

He gulped and stroked her cheek again. "She died, and when she died, my heart died. I can't love you, Addie, and you are a wonderful, special girl who deserves to be loved with all someone's heart. You deserve to have what my Lily had. I can honestly say I wish I could love you like that, but I can't. I can't be what you want me to be, Addie. I can't be the man you deserve. If I were decent, I'd regret… what we did this morning. Apparently, I'm not decent either, because I can't regret it, but I do regret hurting you. That's the last thing I wanted."

Every word dug into her heart, sharp as hammered nails. If words were bullets, she'd be bleeding right now. *Can souls bleed? Mine must be.* She closed her eyes and steeled her resolve.

"If that's how you feel, Jesse," she said with quiet dignity, the only strength she had left in her, "then there's nothing I can do about it. Please give me my things."

"I'll walk you to the door," he offered.

She shook her head. "No. I don't want you to. I want you to ride away and leave me alone. If you care for me at all, you won't make me have some kind of emotional scene in front of an aunt I only know from letters. Ride away, bounty hunter. Don't come back."

"I have to go back to Cañon City, deal with that murderer and his gang. Then I'll come back," Jesse insisted. "I hope by then you'll have found it in your heart to forgive me."

"There's nothing to forgive," Addie replied in her coldest voice, hoping to freeze her own tears to prevent them from escaping. Harsh regret and a touch of hurt burned in Jesse's eyes. "You never gave me any reason to hope for a different outcome. If I made any assumptions about what I meant to you, they're my own fault. There's nothing for you to come back to."

"Addie…" his fingers traced her cheek. Addie stepped back sharply, breaking away from his drugging contact.

"My things, please," she insisted.

Jesse closed his eyes for a moment then nodded and circled her and the horse to the far saddlebag, where he retrieved her possessions.

With nothing to hold them in, they represented an awkward, almost unmanageable bundle, but Addie grimly accepted the stack of clothing and a few personal items and with a nod walked forward. She glanced over her shoulder. "Go on, now. Don't follow me."

"Goodbye, Addie," Jesse said. As she watched, he swung onto Mercury's back, urged the horse to turn, and rode away into the woods, disappearing from view.

Addie took a deep breath and turned, fixing her eyes on the cabin before her. Wishing she had a free hand to wipe her eyes and nose, she steeled herself once more and moved forward.

Leaving the shade of the trees, the pale warmth of the spring sun broke over her and touched the farmstead with golden light, as though a divine presence had settled itself on every surface. *You're never alone,* she reminded herself.

While the property had once clearly been a farm, now the acreage had been converted into a field of flowers. Crocuses bloomed in riotous array, neatly arranged by color, starting with a dark purple closest to the house. A little furrow of earth separated the dark violent from a lighter, brighter shade, and then a deep gold, a pale yellow, some striped varieties, and last, white. The strips of long-stemmed flowers made her smile in spite of her broken heart. *So this is how Auntie Beth makes a living. I wondered.* The plants looked well-tended, with no discolored or insect-chewed leaves. No rot or rust on the petals. Addie took a moment to enjoy the sight and the fresh, spicy scent of the pine trees beyond.

"You there," a deep and melodious female voice rang out across the yard, "those flowers are for sale only. If you want one, you'd best be prepared to pay."

Addie turned on the spot and found herself confronted by a disgruntled-looking woman in her late forties, her red hair loose and flying in the gentle breeze. She had dirt under her fingernails.

"Aunt Beth?" Addie asked.

The woman stopped her tirade abruptly and stared, her tawny eyebrows drawing together. While she looked enough like Addie to make the connection obvious, her eyes were a pale, silver color.

"Adeline?"

"Call me Addie," she responded with a nod.

"Oh, good, Addie. I'm glad you're here. I was starting to worry about you."

"Sorry. I'm here now, and I'm just fine."

The woman moved as though to extend her hand, but then stopped, taking in the loose bundle of fabric clutched in Addie's arms. "Let's get you inside so you can put all that down."

She walked away, her niece trailing along after her, through the yard and a small door into the interior of the cabin. The inside could have been a mirror of the home she'd grown up in, a large room which seemed to comprise parlor, kitchen and dining room all in one. Open doors off the left side and the back revealed small bedrooms, each with a bed which sported a crazy quilt in a pattern of flowers, one mostly in shades of red, the other in blue. More quilts warmed the lath walls and helped muffle the drafts that wanted to creep in at the edges of windows.

They passed two sofas, arranged at right angles to each other, the larger facing an oversized window that revealed a view of the flower garden, the smaller, a red brick fireplace. The wooden arms of the furniture pieces revealed their age, being worn and scratched, but their upholstery remained fresh-looking, in a cozy shade of dark brown. An oil lamp rested on a small, round table. Another, larger table stood behind the seating area, set with four chairs. A bouquet of purple crocuses and white lilacs in a huge vase brought a note of color.

On the right, the kitchen area of a sink with a pump handle, a stove, and a honey-colored icebox. A wooden counter stretched between the appliances, forming a workspace. Cabinets below and shelves above provided storage.

Aunt Beth led Addie straight through to the back, into the bedroom with the blue quilt. The space, though small, more than met Addie's needs, providing a perfectly comfortable looking bed with a delicately-sized wooden headboard, a trunk at the foot of the bed, a wardrobe in the corner, and a mirrored bureau on which rested an oversized white bowl for washing up.

Addie set her mass of clothing down on the bed and turned, at last able to greet the woman who'd been kind enough to provide her a place to stay.

She reached out a hand to Beth, and instead found herself crushed in a warm hug.

"I'm so glad you made it safely here, Addie," Beth said.

"Me too," Addie replied, though she wasn't exactly sure how safe the journey had been, or that she'd arrived unscathed.

Chapter 9

Addie sniffled and pummeled the pillow in mute misery. Her body ached, still recalling the rough way Jesse had used her. Her heart, numb while she'd said goodbye to Jesse, throbbed even more fiercely now that she was alone. She grieved as she'd never grieved in her young life, for her long-dead mother, her recently lost father, her first love's abandonment, and the most painful of all, for herself, for the innocence and hope that had colored her view of the world up to this point.

Disillusioned by too much loss, Addie pressed her mouth into the pillow and sobbed. Not with hysterical tears, but with the long, soul-deep whimpers of agonized despair. *What life will I have now? What future? I wish I had died with my father and spared myself this.*

Giving herself over to her misery, Addie wept long into the night.

Jesse stared into his campfire, watching the flames lick at the kindling. *Perhaps in the fire, I can find the answer to how life can be this way. Why did I lose an angel only to abandon a good woman? What's wrong with me?* He hurt. The weasels were back, chewing on his guts. He felt sick with shame. *If I can't love Addie, why did I have to want her? Why did I harm a good girl? For lust? Has this wild way of life finally damaged my soul?*

Knowing he'd never hurt an innocent so badly, he grieved. Grieved for Addie's lost innocence, a loss he'd perpetrated on her. He would never forget the look of agony on her face when he left her at her aunt's house. She'd tried so hard to be stoic, but couldn't conceal the pain.

Some friend you turned out to be. For shame, Jesse West. Shame was right. Shame wrapped around him like a blanket. Shame turned his heart to ice. *I don't deserve a woman like Addie. My actions prove I never deserved Lily either.* And yet, what could he do now to fix it? Only what he had done.

The pounding on Addie's door matched the pounding in her head. She groaned as the sunlight assaulted her swollen eyes.

"Addie?" Beth's voice cut through, "Are you okay? It's almost noon."

Noon? Oh no! "Sorry, Aunt Beth. Yes, I'm okay. I'll be out in a minute."

"Okay," Beth replied. "There's coffee here and I was going to fix up some chicken soup."

"That sounds good," Addie called, groaning as she dragged herself from the bed. As she pulled on bloomers and a simple gray dress, her stockings and boots, she imagined wrapping her Kiowa acceptance of life and suffering, grief, pain and death around her like a cloak. It settled on her wounded heart, not staunching the flow of misery, but muffling it, allowing her to put one foot in front of another.

"Are you sure you're all right?" Beth asked as Addie stepped outside the bedroom door.

"Yes," Addie replied.

"Loss hurts."

Oh please, don't sympathize. I'm holding on by a thread! "I'm fine," Addie said again, her voice flat.

Beth nodded. "I understand. If you feel like you need to cry, I for one won't tell you otherwise. Listen to yourself, Addie, so you can heal and move on."

I'll never move on from this. Never. But somehow, she had to, had to pack up the broken pieces that had once been her heart and move forward, not to love or marriage or family, but at least to something like a regular life. "Thank you for letting me stay with you, Beth. I want to earn my keep. What can I do to help?"

"Actually, Addie, I was hoping you'd help me with my business. During the growing season, I sell flowers for church altar decorations, weddings, funerals, all that. In the winter, I sew quilts, and also make pine wreaths and garland. I know from your letters that you're good with plants."

Addie slowly tipped and raised her chin. "I can do that."

"So tell me," Beth continued, making idle conversation, "how did you get here? You didn't come all this way alone, did you?"

"No," Addie replied, pouring coffee into a blue tin mug. "A friend of my father's escorted me."

She glanced at Beth. Her aunt was regarding her with a questioning expression.

"His name is Jesse West," Addie offered, but her heart clenched painfully even mentioning the name of her faithless lover, and she made no further comment. After a while, Beth shrugged and went on about her business, leaving Addie to brood into her cup of coffee.

Jesse rode Mercury out of town, returning the spot where the bandit had attacked Addie. With a disgusted sigh, he lowered a rope and hauled the bloody remains of the man up from the bottom of the cliff, wrapping him in the remaining blanket. *I hope there's a reward. There's no way I'm using this one again.* Laying the stiffened bundle across the horse's back, he pondered his next move.

The temperature had dropped further, in that uncertain way March was known to do, and he huddled deeper in his coat. The leather of the reins slipped and slid through the leather of his gloves. His eyes and nose stung with the cold, and his cheeks felt like fire as he fought forward through a driving wind.

Riding would be so much easier, but he had no desire to share space on the horse's back with the stiffened, contorted corpse. *I just want to get to town as quickly as possible.*

Urging Mercury to move faster, Jesse crested a hill and left Colorado Springs behind him, heading back into Cañon City to deliver the body and find out if any reward had been offered. Then it would be back into the mountains to seek his prey. While he knew the man who had accosted them had not acted alone, he had no idea under whose authority the man had operated, nor what their objectives were. As he walked, the thoughts clicked and clattered in his mind, trying to fit together into a coherent whole.

He was quick, resourceful and violent, but not clever. He let slip he was part of a group. He underestimated Addie. A clever man would have been on guard against those things. He didn't have leadership qualities.

An underling, but a high-level one. Someone else was holding his leash. Someone who could manipulate, but probably lacked physical strength. A man who is physically strong and manipulative does his own missions. He wouldn't trust an underling unless it was necessary.

So we have a smart leader who is physically less than imposing and a strong but not too clever second. Are there more? There would be more. Two men could easily have fled, moved camp. It would have to be a large group and a wanted one to risk an assassination rather than waiting… or hiding. There was every chance he and Addie had stumbled across a major operation on that mountain. *Probably too many for me to take them alone.*

He urged Mercury on towards Cañon City.

"Addie," Beth called. "Are there any daffodils left?"

"I'll look," Addie called back, wrapping a shawl around her shoulders and stepping out into the brisk March air. In the week she'd been with her aunt, she'd been learning how to run a flower business. While she knew a great deal about how to use plants, she'd never tried selling them.

It's early for a wedding. I wonder if there's a funeral. It was hard to feel much emotional attachment either way. Though she'd met quite a few people when her aunt took her to town, and to church last Sunday, she didn't know anyone well, and still felt powerfully alone.

A quick glance at the flowers told her everything she needed to know. Shivering, she hurried back into the house.

"There are enough left to make one bouquet and maybe three or four purple crocuses for contrast."

"I thought so," Beth replied. "But never mind that. If the daffodils had been used up, there would have been plenty of other colors of crocuses to make a bouquet.

"I don't want colored flowers," a whiny-sounding voice complained. "I came for white."

Addie regarded the girl sitting at the kitchen table with her aunt. She appeared quite young. Maybe even a couple years younger than Addie. *Not a funeral then, it looks like. Could it be a wedding? If so, some poor boy is in for an unpleasant surprise.*

"Rachael, this is my niece, Adeline McCoy."

Addie nodded to the girl. "Well, if you need the flowers right away, you're in luck. As I just said, there are enough left for one bouquet."

"Well, what are you waiting for then? Go get them," the girl snapped as though she were talking to an imbecile.

"Now hold on there, Rachael," Beth urged. "We don't want to pick them too far in advance. When do you need them?"

"Tomorrow," Rachael replied. "I know you heard about it. Everyone has heard about it."

"Sorry." Beth shook her head and Addie followed suit. She had no idea what was going on.

"I'm getting married tomorrow at two. I want a bouquet of flowers."

"Of course," Beth replied. "I'll make up the bouquet and bring it to you tomorrow at the church. Does that sound all right?"

The girl rolled her eyes. "What else would you do?"

Beth refused to take offense. "I'll be there at one. Addie, would you please get my account book? It's on my bureau. When you get a chance, pull out one of the old quilts from the garden shed. We'll need to cover the flowers tonight to be sure they don't freeze. I'm afraid a cold snap is brewing."

Nodding, Addie hurried to comply. *Brides are insane,* she thought to herself. *Maybe it's a good thing I'll never be one.*

Planning the raid on the mountain stronghold had taken the better part of a week.

Now all the planning had been completed, and the posse, sitting on horses, bristling with shotguns and pistols, shifted nervously in the yard of Anne's boarding house, waiting for the order to head out. Jesse had found the Sheriff of Cañon City more than ready to cooperate, and the two of them had put together a posse.

Careful questioning of people who had been involved in various criminal activities had revealed a gang of at least thirty men. Jesse assumed they must be heavily armed if the knife and gun the bandit had used on Addie was any indication. *Thank God my girl is so resourceful.*

Angrily he pushed the thought away. *Addie is not your girl. Just because you stole a taste doesn't mean anything.* He didn't want to acknowledge that something had changed the first time she'd put her sweet lips on his. Though when Anne's lush, curvy body had slipped into his bed three nights ago, placing his hands on her generous breasts, he'd failed to rise to the occasion. *Focus, West. Losing focus gets a man killed on missions like this.*

"Fall in!" the sheriff called, smoothing his black handlebar mustache. "Remember your instructions, men. Follow me."

He spurred his horse and the posse rode for the mountain pass, ready to do battle with an unknown band of murderous criminals.

Ugh, Addie thought to herself, *the mercantile stinks today. Too many unwashed mountain men.* The rank stink of sweat and horse, along with the foul odor of a wet dog who sat shivering miserably near the fire assaulted the girl's nose. After delivering the wedding flowers to the church in a chilly downpour, Beth and Addie had decided to wait out the storm in the store, where a cup of hot coffee and a plate of pastries made by the owner's wife provided a pleasant means to pass the time.

Addie sipped her coffee and surveyed the motley characters who clustered around the stove, trying to escape the biting humidity. *This mountain grows some rugged folk.* She spotted a boot with a hole through which the wearer's two toes had escaped, a pair of ragged britches with a hole in one buttock which allowed the man's red union suit to show through, and an unlovely assortment of other torn and faded clothing wrapped around the bodies of equally faded men. Of other women, there was no sign. *Probably all at the wedding.*

The door slammed open, setting the little bell above ringing with great violence and a huge, shaggy specimen of a man stomped in. Addie's eyes widened at the sight. Great masses of curly black hair streamed from beneath a ragged knitted cap. Wild black brows clustered above equally wild black eyes. The man's nose was broad and flat, his lips completely concealed behind a massive beard that straggled halfway down his barrel chest, ending just where his belly pushed slightly against his belt buckle.

"Bear!" Someone shouted, and the man with the hole in his boot hurried to escort the new arrival to a spot by the fire.

Bear? They sure called that one right! As the hairy fellow approached the fire, the stink of too many bodies finally drove Addie out onto the porch. A cold place to wait, but at least the air smelled clean.

This afternoon, Beth promised to show me how to make a wildflower nosegay. I can't wait. The chicken and dumplings simmering on the stove seemed to call to her as well. *Hurry, Beth. Please hurry. I don't want to be here anymore.* At least in the little cabin, there would be peace.

The acrid tang of gunpowder smoke and the thick sweat of stressed, nervous men stung Jesse's nose and caused his eyes to water. Men and horses ran screaming through the melee. Shotguns blasted and pistols roared. To Jesse's ears, the sound seemed muffled. His gaze was fixed on the abandoned farmstead which had become home base for no less than forty bandits.

Thankfully the posse had discovered the weapons stockpile in a crumbling outbuilding before their adversaries could get there. That meant much fewer guns and bullets in the hands of their enemies, though the criminals were far from unarmed.

Off to Jesse's left, two men hid, one behind a decaying wagon, the other on the side of a boulder, occasionally popping out to fire shots at each other. Straight ahead, two men were taking turns kicking the front door of the farmhouse, trying to access the criminals hiding inside.

To the right, one of the posse members took a bullet to the leg and fell screaming. Jesse didn't engage in the action. He constantly scanned the scene, looking for the man he felt would be the boss. *Obvious leadership abilities, but not physically strong. An unimposing specimen with an inflated sense of his own value.* His eyes touched each man, wondering which one was the culprit. *I don't think he's here. Could he have gotten wind that we were coming?*

Jesse pushed forward in a sudden burst, dodging to avoid a knife thrown in his direction, ducking under the swing of a shotgun barrel. *The leader would be in the safest place. That would be inside... not the house. He'd be somewhere less obvious. Somewhere he could disappear and wait out the action, while still keeping an eye on things.*

Jesse slipped behind a tree and scanned his surroundings again. *Hiding in plain sight. Present, yet invisible. Where can you hide on a farmstead? Anywhere... like there.* He zeroed in on a storm cellar, the door standing open. *Now I have you.* Instead of crossing the danger zone between the fence and the farmhouse, Jesse skirted the scene, keeping to the woods, approaching the cellar by stealth.

Training a shotgun into the opening, he yelled, "I know you're in there. Come out, and keep your hands where I can see 'em! His words echoed into the cavernous space. *That's too much echo for a storm cellar. Could they have expanded it? Do I dare go in there alone?*

A strange movement caught his eyes from several yards distant. Another door like the one standing before him swung upwards, showering concealing leaves in all directions. Two men exited. One was beefy with a head like a melon. *Another lackey.* Jesse dismissed him instantly. The second figure was small and slight and walked with a decided limp. He wore what even from this distance could be recognized as an expensive black suit and a top hat.

"You there, stop!" Jesse called. The men froze and whirled, the bulky one whipping out a pistol. At this distance, dodging the bullet required little effort, but it did afford the pair enough time to retrieve two horses hidden in the forest and bolt off toward the horizon.

"Damn it!" Jesse cursed. "This isn't over," he muttered before turning back to the farmyard where the posse had clearly overcome the surprised gang and was beginning to round them up.

Part II

Chapter 10

Four months later.

"Ad-die," Beth called in a melodious voice. "Addie, where are you? I have news."

Huddled miserably in the shade of a large evergreen, Addie gagged, wiped her mouth and tried to will herself to stop vomiting. She did not succeed.

"Addie, are you here?"

A hot, dry wind blew over her sweaty forehead and cut through her dress, pelting her with dust.

"Oh, Addie," Beth said, placing a hand on the back of her neck.

How does she stay so cool in the heat? The touch soothed the girl and at last, her gagging subsided.

"Come on, honey, get up. Let's get you back inside. I'll make you some tea to settle your stomach."

Moving slowly so as not to upset her still protesting guts any further, Addie shuffled into the house. *What will happen now? Will she throw me out? Will I have to make my way alone... and not alone? What will become of us?* Panic nearly sent her churning belly into open revolt. Swallowing convulsively, she allowed Beth to lead her to the sofa near the window. Addie shivered and took slow, deep breaths, trying to squelch the urge to gag. *If you start again, you might not be able to stop. Remember the last time?* The last time when she'd gagged and heaved for nearly an hour before she could get control of herself.

Pushing all thought away, Addie stared blankly into the woods, watching the fragrant pines dance around in a hot, stale breeze while Beth clanked and clattered as she puttered around in the kitchen.

In a surprisingly short amount of time, not even enough for Addie to stop shuddering completely, a delicate china cup filled with unsweetened black tea landed in her hands. Ignoring manners and finesse, she clutched the cup and lifted it unsteadily to her lips.

"Don't you think it's about time," Beth said gently, "to admit you're in a family way, sweetie?"

Addie squeezed her eyes shut and dipped her chin in a single, miserable nod.

Beth laid a hand on Addie's back, rubbing up and down. "Try not to panic. I know how scary this is."

"You do?" Addie met her aunt's eyes and saw moisture sparkling in the corners. Beth smiled a sad, sad smile.

"Yes. When I was sixteen, a boy told me he loved me and then took advantage of me."

"He didn't…" Addie interrupted, but Beth held up her hand, asking for patience.

"When my parents found out, they gave me two choices. I could go to the home for unwed mothers and they would allow me to come back… after. Or I could leave for good."

Addie gulped. Was that the choice Beth was presenting her? Her heart clenched.

"I have no doubt what I would have ended up doing if I'd chosen to leave, and I didn't want that. So I went to the home." The sorrow in Beth's eyes told the rest of the story.

"That must have been horrible," Addie said, biting down on her lower lip.

Beth nodded. "It was," she replied, "but it was probably the best option for the child. Now he… or she has a real family."

"You don't even know what you had?" Addie gasped.

Beth slowly turned her head from side to side. "The workers believed not knowing would help us let go, try to live normal lives again. My baby was whisked away seconds after delivery and I was packed off home two weeks later."

Addie considered this. The jolt of raw agony that tore through her insides told her what she needed to know about that option.

"I won't do it," she said firmly.

"You don't have to," Beth replied. "I didn't think you would, but I want to help you think through your options. No matter what you choose there will be hard things to deal with, and you need to know what they will be. The home for unwed mothers is one option. It's painful, but sometimes it's best. I wouldn't fault anyone for going that route. You can also stay here. I'm willing, and the flower and quilt business would probably stretch to provide for one more, now that I have you to help me, but you have to realize, Addie, that everyone will know. That will be hard for you because there will be gossip. It will be hard for your little one as well, growing up as the town bastard."

Beth paused and Addie took a few slow, deep breaths, taking in the information, trying to make the shattered pieces of her mind form coherent thoughts.

At last, Addie met Beth's gaze again. "What else?"

"You could leave. Relocate to another town. Tell people you're a widow, try to find work, or create it. You might also find a husband."

"That would involve lying for the rest of my life, including to my husband. I don't like lying." *And I don't much want a husband either. Particularly not under these circumstances.*

"I know," Beth agreed, "but there's no point leaving if you're not willing to."

Addie acknowledged that with the tip of her chin.

"I think the best idea, though, is to contact Jesse and let him know what happened. If it's true he didn't take advantage, that things got out of control, don't you think you should tell him? Give him the chance to do the right thing?"

"What makes you say it was Jesse? How do you know I didn't have a liaison with someone back in my hometown?" Addie challenged, assuaging her pain by lashing out at Beth.

The woman took no offense. *Beth lets everything roll off her. I like that about her.*

"I know from several things, honey. First, I heard about that terrible bastard you were betrothed to, and I know it wasn't him. If you'd met someone else, you'd have stayed and gotten married, not come all this way. Second, I saw how sad you were when you arrived, and the look in your eyes whenever you mentioned Jesse. He's more than a family friend to you, and I'd bet my last piece of peach pie on it. Am I wrong?"

"You're not wrong," Addie mumbled, turning to face the window. She no longer felt hot, and the chill in her heart seemed to be spreading.

"Maybe you should write to Jesse then," Beth suggested.

Addie shook her head. "I don't want to be anyone's responsibility."

Beth laughed.

Addie whipped her head around to glare at her.

"Is that what you think? You think you need Jesse to take care of you? Honey, that's not what I meant at all. His responsibility, both of your responsibilities, is to take care of that baby, give it the best possible life. You know what it's like for illegitimate children out there. No child should have to face that if the option is there."

"I don't know where he is," Addie said, tossing up her last objection. "His job takes him all over. He could be in Colorado, Kansas or even Nebraska right now chasing down criminals."

"He's about a half-mile down the road, in that old mill that's been converted into a rooming house."

Addie froze. Her eyebrows drew together and her jaw dropped. "What?"

Beth nodded, her lips twisting into a smug smile. "He rented a room there and apart from the odd week or two on the road, hasn't gone anywhere."

Addie stared, aghast. "How do you know?" She met her aunt's eyes, making no attempt to hide her disbelief.

"He contacted me," Beth replied, looking contrite. "As soon as he got back from… well from taking care of some business in Cañon City, he sent me a note. We've been corresponding ever since."

Addie's eyebrows drew together in a puzzled expression. "All this time? It's been months."

Beth nodded. "I know. He wants to be sure you're safe. He says it's because he promised your father, but I have my doubts. He knows you're safe with me. He can't let you go, Addie, any more than you could forget him. That's why I think talking to him would be best."

Addie shook her head hard, trying to make sense of what she was hearing. The movement caused her unsettled belly to lurch and she groaned.

"Easy, honey," Beth urged. "I hope you get past the sick part soon. You should be about done."

"I hope so," Addie replied, clutching her churning stomach. *Breathe, Addie. Keep breathing slowly. Focus on the conversation.* "Why didn't you tell me about Jesse?"

"You weren't ready," Beth replied. "You were still too angry. You think I don't recognize the signs? I know what it looks like when a girl and her lover have a falling out. I know how hard it is to get past the hurt feelings. I planned to tell you soon, but it looks like soon has become now."

"So you knew all along that Jesse and I had been… intimate?" Addie blushed, but the burning in her cheeks distracted her from her nausea, so she didn't mind.

"I had a strong suspicion, especially after I met him. Such a handsome young man… and so kind. And before you ask," Beth held up one hand, seeing Addie was about to interrupt, "he asked me not to mention seeing him or talking to him."

"What do you think he has in mind?" Addie asked. "Why on earth would he hang around town here and never say a word to me? What does he want?" The thought of seeing Jesse caused hysteria to flare in Addie.

Beth laid a calming hand on her niece's arm. "I don't think he knew himself, Addie. He tried to explain his reasoning to me. It sounded like a lot of hogwash, typical male heroism played out all wrong. I tried to tell him, but he wouldn't listen. Stubborn as a mule, that one."

Addie grinned without humor. *You don't know the half of it, Aunt Beth.*

"But yet he can't make himself leave," the older woman continued. "He loves you. I know he does. He's just being stupid about it."

Addie recalled her dream. How her mother had urged patience and persistence. She'd never guessed so much would be required, but if what Beth was saying was true, she'd given up far too soon. *Water shaping rock. I walked away at the first sign of resistance.* Chastened at her own flightiness, Addie considered seriously, for the first time, telling Jesse about the baby, their baby. The baby he'd planted in her because the thought of her death had overcome his restraint.

But he humiliated me. He bedded me and dropped me off and left without so much as a backward glance. The memory burned, hot and painful. "I can't go to Jesse, I just can't," Addie whined, clutching her forehead in one hand.

"Why not?" Beth demanded.

"He doesn't love me."

"Bullshit," the Beth exclaimed, and her obscenity arrested Addie's attention. "He loves you. If he didn't love you, he wouldn't be hanging around this town when there are escaped convicts all over the mountains waiting to be brought to justice, with rewards offered. If he didn't love you, he wouldn't have brought you here with everything unsettled. He'd have played smooth and suave with you, and then left without another word. Did he do that, Addie?"

"No," she admitted. "He tried so hard not to let this happen. Tried to warn me not to get too close to him."

"Tried not to let it happen how? By pulling out? That doesn't work, Addie."

Addie choked on a sip of her rapidly cooling tea. "Auntie! No, not like that. He didn't want to take my virginity, wanted me to save it for the mythical man who was supposed to become my husband. It was only when my life was threatened that he… we lost control."

"Tell me that doesn't all sound like love, Addie," Beth said dryly.

Addie studied the grain of one of the floorboards. "He was in love with a girl named Lily. She died."

"That doesn't mean he can never love again. Are you willing to let him cherish his memories of Lily?"

"I don't think it's different from me cherishing memories of Mama and Dad, right?"

"Right," Beth agreed. "The passing of those we love changes us, makes us who we are. We shouldn't regret that. So are you going to contact Jesse?"

Addie closed her eyes and searched deep within herself. She considered the options and their impact on herself and the tiny person growing inside her. Pressing her hand to her abdomen, she felt the slight swelling that had only recently begun to strain the seams of her bloomers. She imagined Jesse. Aunt Beth was right about one thing. He'd take responsibility.

She doubted he'd resent her either. She imagined the tiny swell grown, as it soon would, to a heavy roundness. Imagined lying beside Jesse in a comfortable bed, his arms around her waist, his hand on her belly, his hot breath on the back of her neck. Whether he ever admitted he loved her, at least he could touch her again, could hold her close. She wasn't taking him from anyone who might need or deserve him. It wouldn't harm him.

"Yes," she said at last, and the decision filled her with peace.

"Do you want me with you?" Beth asked. "Or would you rather have some privacy? I've been meaning to take a little trip out of town and visit a friend of mine in Denver, and I haven't been on the train in ages, so if you don't mind being on your own a few days, I could do that, but I have no problem staying close to home either." Beth's eyes shone when she spoke of the trip.

Something more is going on in your head, Aunt Beth, and I aim to get to the bottom of it. But for the moment, Addie had her own issues to deal with. Still, she couldn't help but smile. "Go on your trip. I'll be fine. One thing I'm sure about. Jesse would never harm me."

"That's good to hear," Beth said. "Why don't you get changed, and then write that letter. We need to go into town anyway."

"All right," Addie replied.

Chapter 11

The main street of Colorado Springs consisted of a row of adjoined buildings, painted in bright colors. At the end of the street, the mountains raised white heads like grizzled potentates against the horizon. Clouds massed and roiled in the sky above, turning the vivid blue of July to an ominous slate gray. Rain felt imminent, and indeed, the crisp, sharp scent of impending showers hung in the still air. Addie clutched her umbrella tight in her hand and shivered.

"Addie, Addie!" A rumbling voice called. Addie rolled her eyes and ducked into the mercantile, pretending not to see the towering, bear-like man trailing her. *I wish he would give up already.*

Inside the general store, two men sat near a cold potbellied stove, playing checkers and trying not to get caught cheating. Three ladies in gray skirts and colorful coats stood gossiping near the cash register while their children gazed hopefully into the candy display, their faces pressed against the glass. Addie passed everyone with polite nods and handed the letter to the store owner, who also happened to be the postman. He took the envelope without a second glance, leaving Addie free to browse. A skein of soft white yarn snared her eye and she touched the skein with one fingertip. *I could knit that into the sweetest blanket.*

"Addie, there you are!"

Sighing, Addie turned, taking in the towering form of a man, well above six feet tall, thickset and bulky with a shock of wild, curly hair streaming down around his shoulders in back and obscuring his eyes in the front. An equally dense beard clung to his cheeks. "I don't recall giving you leave to use my Christian name, Mr. Mills," she replied in her coldest voice.

"So coy," he commented, as though she were playing a game with him. "I like that."

How stupid can one man be? Addie didn't bother to respond. Instead, she turned and slowly stalked away.

"Addie!" he grabbed her arm.

She whirled with a hiss. "Let me go. Take your hand off me." She yanked against his grip but to no avail. His fingers clutched like iron and refused to release.

"Settle down, Miss Addie," the man said in a gentle voice under which his steely determination peeked like a hidden rattlesnake. "Let's just take a seat on the bench outside and have a little talk."

Her heart pounding, Addie tried once more to wrench her arm free from the man's grip, but to no avail. His fingers tightened until she could feel her skin bruising. Though she could probably escape by injuring him, she didn't want to make a scene. *Not to mention, I don't want to incite him. He gives me such an unsettled feeling. I'm sure he's prone to violence.* She didn't want violence to touch her, especially now that she knew she was pregnant.

She let the oversized beast lead her out into the cloudy heat, planting her roughly on the bench and joining her before she could flee. He captured her hand and laced his meaty fingers through it.

"I've been real nice to you, Miss Addie," he said in a sad but also threatening voice, "and you've been a bitch to me. That will stop now. I want to court you and I expect you to let me do it, you hear?"

"But listen, Mr. Mills," Addie insisted, and his hand tightened painfully on her fingers. One of her knuckles popped.

"Call me Byron… or rather Bear. My friends call me Bear."

What friends, you oversized shoe brush? "I'm sorry, but I'm not interested in being courted at this time, and I don't think we're a good match. Please, don't take it the wrong way. I'm sure for the right girl, you'd be a great catch." *If the right girl lives in the woods and tears apart beehives with her fingernails.*

"You're too sassy by half," Bear snarled, looking and sounding like his name-sake. "You should be glad I'm willing to take you on. You'll be a proper lady once I'm through training you."

Addie shuddered. She wanted to know neither his idea of a proper lady nor his training methods.

"I'm not yours to train, Mr. Mills." She wrenched her hand again. Lulled by her apparent passivity, his relaxed fingers were unable to clamp down on hers. "I don't know what you think makes someone a lady, but being rough and forceful sure doesn't make you a gentleman."

He grabbed for her but she dodged. "Hear me now. I am *not* interested in being courted by you, now or ever. I don't want to be your girl. I don't want to be trained by you. In fact, you can leave me alone."

The hefty man surged to his feet and lunged. Addie drove the toe of her boot into his shin. Bear yelped and in that moment of distraction Addie whipped her knife out of her boot, waving it under her adversary's nose. "No means no, Mr. Mills," she said in a cold, stern voice. "Even when you don't agree. Do not assume everyone small is helpless."

Backing slowly away from the man, keeping her knife poised, she made her way to Aunt Beth's buggy, where Rosie the patient mule waited to bring them and their purchases back from town. Beth was already waiting, and Addie scrambled into the buggy, trying not to turn her back on Bear for a second. Though he was already distant, she kept an eye on the dark, shaggy figure. A space between her shoulder blades itched. *This isn't finished.*

"Ha," Beth said, shaking the reins, and the mule trotted forward. "Now then, my dearest, what the hell just happened?"

Addie smiled, amused by her aunt's dirty mouth, but tension stilled strummed through her. "Bear Mills," she replied in her usual succinct way.

At last, with the mercantile no longer visible, she consented to turn around and face the mountain in front of them, letting the sight of the peak soothe her nerves.

"Good Lord," Beth sighed. "Is that oversized bully still lurking around? I thought they were going to ship him out."

"Still around, and apparently he's sweet on me." Addie rolled her eyes.

"Get out, really?"

"Yep."

Beth shuddered. "I don't know about you, but personally I'd rather go to bed with a porcupine than that big dolt."

Addie giggled. "You have that right."

Then Beth grew serious. "He's not taking no for an answer?"

"Nope," Addie concurred. "I had to be… quite forceful to get away from him."

"That's not good. Maybe I should stay close. Two shotguns are better than one."

Addie sighed and massaged her aching temples, and then her belly. Nausea was trying to rise again. "No, go. I need some time with Jesse to talk to him, see what he wants to do. Besides, I think your friend is a gentleman who would like to see you." She risked a glance at Beth and saw a smile on her aunt's face, her weathered cheeks turning pink with pleasure.

"By the way," Beth added, changing the subject, "I got a note that might interest you. Remember all those letters you sent me over the years? The ones about plants and their uses?"

"Sure," Addie replied, recalling how often she'd written to her aunt about the edible and medicinal fauna of Colorado. "Why?"

"Well, I thought they deserved to be known. I took a risk and sent one to a newspaper in Denver, under a man's name, of course. They're interested and would like to run a weekly column, and they'll pay you a little. Not enough to live on, sadly, but enough to help out, if you're interested. I hope you don't mind."

Addie considered. Should something go wrong with Jesse and she and Beth have to raise the baby alone, a little extra income would be welcome. While her help made the flower and quilt-making business her aunt ran out of their cabin home more efficient and profitable, being able to contribute more would go a long way toward making her feel useful. She nodded. "That would be very nice. Thank you, Beth."

"Of course, Addie."

"I'm glad I came here," the girl commented. "It's nicer than being alone. You've shown me so many things I would never have realized. Especially with the…" she laid her fingertips on her belly. "Most guardians wouldn't have been so accepting, so I'm doubly glad."

Beth patted her knee. "I remember what it's like, Addie. I'm also glad I was here to help you. You would have made your way somehow, I have no doubt, but some things are best not done alone."

Addie nodded.

"So when did you ask for Jesse to come and talk to you?"

Addie toyed with one of the buttons on her jacket. "It seems so strange that he's living right down the road and I can't just go to him."

"I know, but that's a rooming house for men only. If you went there, it would look bad, and no one could guarantee your safety. Besides, Bear lives there too."

"Definitely not then." Addie shuddered. "I suppose the letter will take a few days to reach him. I asked him to come by Sunday morning. All the customers who want to order flowers will be in church. No idlers or busybodies hanging around."

"Good thought." Beth shook the reins to help the mule keep moving. Rosie was showing signs of wanting to snuffle a pine tree. "I can probably get a spot on tomorrow's train and be back in a week or so. You all right being alone that long?"

Addie chuckled. "Auntie, when the old pastor and his wife moved away, I'd be alone for months on end while Dad worked. I can manage a week."

"How is it you never had any trouble? Didn't anyone think they might try something since you were a young girl by yourself?"

Addie blushed a bit to recall how Ed had sometimes come to visit, back before their falling out. They had most definitely gotten into trouble. Not to the extent she and Jesse had, but there had been more than a little indiscreet touching. "Someone did try once. Got as far as the edge of the property before the racket in the barn got my attention."

"Really?" Beth's eyes grew huge. "What did you do? How did you protect yourself?"

"The fool was wearing a red plaid shirt," Addie replied, "and stood out like a cardinal in the snow. I shot him with buckshot from the porch of the house. At that distance, I knew it wouldn't do any permanent harm, but a backside full of shot convinced him to leave me alone. I mean, it's a small town. People knew I was a tomboy. Most of the younger ones had seen me gut a fish, and also had seen me take down a bully who pulled my hair at school. I don't think anyone conceived of me as an easy target."

"Atta girl," Beth said, an approving smile carving pleasant grooves around her mouth. "You're very much one of us, Adeline McCoy."

"That's right," Addie agreed. "McCoy women: little bundles of trouble and sass."

"You sound like an advertisement," Beth laughed.

"You think? Maybe we could both catch husbands with it."

Chuckling, they continued joking back and forth all the way back to the cabin. Addie's enjoyment didn't entirely stop the churning in her belly, but taking her mind off it went a long way towards keeping it from growing to an uncontrollable level.

The ladies spent the evening baking cookies and chatting while Beth packed her bag to visit her friend. A secret smile curved her lips the whole time, and Addie knew it was a gentleman she was going to see. *Scandalous.* The thought made Addie grin.

"So, what's his name?" she asked Beth as she scooped the cinnamon sugar balls from the baking sheet.

"Who?" Beth asked, playing dumb.

"Your 'friend'."

Beth blushed. "Bill," she muttered.

"Do you love Bill?" Addie pressed. *Beth knows all my secrets. I wish I knew a bit more about her.*

The pinkness in Beth's cheeks darkened. "Maybe," she replied.

"Oh, I think you do," Addie teased. Finished with the cookies, she licked a bit of spiced sugar from the tip of one finger. "I think you're mad for him. What's he like?"

"Nice," Beth replied.

Addie rolled her eyes. "Is that the best you can do?"

Beth sighed. "Fine, nosy girl. Yes, I think I am in love with Bill. We met when he came to town on business—he's a newspaper reporter and he was doing a series of articles on towns along the borders of various states and territories. He interviewed me, and when the interview was done, he took me to lunch. We had a pleasant conversation and then began corresponding. This was about four years ago."

"Four *years*?!"

Beth nodded.

"How do you stand it?"

"I insisted. Addie, people sometimes assume I'm easy. That boy when I was sixteen wasn't my only lover. I was quite wild in my twenties, but as the years went by, I had decided to… stop all that. So with Bill, I took it slow. We corresponded for a year before we ever saw each other again, and then we met as friends. To be honest, we didn't become intimate until about six months ago. Bill is a true gentleman, but even his considerable patience has its limits."

Addie smiled. "Sounds like a keeper."

Beth smiled, but not as widely as her niece had expected.

"What's wrong?" Addie asked.

"He's definitely a keeper, but I don't know if I'm someone he should be keeping. He's a well-respected man in his town. He's moved up recently from reporter to editor. The owner of the paper is retiring soon, and Bill is in line to take over. He's been studying, training and preparing for years. I don't think it will do him any good to be seen with a foul-mouthed tart five years his senior."

"Bullshit," Addie retorted, borrowing one of Beth's favorite swearwords. "You're not a tart. I won't argue foul-mouthed, but you might be able to control that a bit out in public, and I'm sure you've slipped in front of him once or twice, right?"

Beth rolled her eyes. "Once or twice an hour."

Addie chuckled. "I'm sure that's true. So he knows what he's getting into. Let him make the decision."

"Are you suggesting I marry him?" Beth demanded. "Not that he's asked, but where would we live? My flower farm is here. I can't very well move it to Denver just to be close to him, and the newspaper here isn't looking for a new owner. We're stuck in our respective places."

"I don't know all the answers," Addie said, "but I know that not being with the person you love hurts."

"That it does," Beth agreed. "That it does."

Jesse sprawled on the hard, wooden-seated armchair in his room. He regarded the view through the window of mountains beyond. He would have to leave soon, get out there and hunt down another bail jumper, or he was going to run out of money. It wasn't free, this tiny room he was living in. Not to mention Mercury's spot in the barn, the horse's food, his own meager meals, all had a cost, and his savings were critically low.

The breeze stirred the bare branches of a small oak outside the window. They scraped against the glass, setting Jesse's teeth on edge. *I have to leave. Tomorrow. I can't stay here anymore. I don't know why I'm still here.* But he did know. He knew without a doubt what anchored him to this spot and refused to release him.

Big brown eyes. Soft, burnished hair. Petite, curvy figure. Smart mouth. Smart woman. Jesse shook his head, fighting to clear out the images. Instead, he focused on a perfect blond. *Lily looked like an angel even when she was alive. Wait... were her eyes sky blue, wolf blue, or slightly greenish like the water in a mountain lake? Were her lips a perfect Cupid's bow, or a bit fuller?* Day by day, Lily was slipping away from him. Heaven was claiming her memories, the last part of her he had.

Addie had distracted him with her quiet observation, her intelligent conversation and her blistering sexuality. She interfered with his perfect grief, made a little corner of the scar that had once been his heart want to beat again. *Warm and vital and strong. Nothing can wear this woman down. I admire her. So what?* He'd meant what he said about female friends. That they'd once crossed the line and become lovers shouldn't destroy that.

But it will. Because like it or not, Addie loves you, you pig.

To distract himself, he opened the first of the letters he'd received that day. A slow smile spread across his face as he saw Kristina's distinctive handwriting. The letter was dated seven months past, before Christmas. Sometimes he could be a bit hard to track down.

> Dear Jesse,
>
> I hope you are well and that you are enjoying many adventures. Life in Garden is progressing like it always has... well almost. We have a new pastor for the church. Dad's been preaching since the poor old Pastor passed away. This new fellow is far too young and more than a little too bossy for my taste. Tries to lead the choir, poor man, though he has little musical talent and even less training. It will be a Christmas miracle if we get the pageant ready in time. I think he might like Ilse Jackson. What a shame that would be. Can you imagine Ilse as a pastor's wife? I shudder to think it!
>
> In other news, there are train robbers in Southwest Kansas. I hope they don't come this way. They've shot people. It's really scary. Maybe it's good I have nowhere to go.
>
> Sorry to cut this short, Jesse, but the organ is calling me. You know how it is. Nothing like Christmas carols to make one feel like playing. Or maybe you don't. Regardless, be careful out there, and come visit now and again. Say hello to Mercury for me.
>
> Kristina

Jesse chuckled throughout the letter. Something about the way Kristina wrote about the pastor made him wonder whether she was sweet on him. Maybe Kris had finally had her eye snared. He hoped so, but only if the young pastor was worth the trouble. *Those damned train robbers keep popping up in conversation...I wonder, could it be the same nest of fools I helped root out near Cañon City? We got most of them, but at least a dozen got away.* Jesse scowled.

Setting aside his friend's missive, he tore open the second envelope. This was from Wesley Fulton, another close friend. It was dated two weeks prior. The letter had a noticeably terse tone.

> *Jesse,*
>
> *In the last few months, we've had a lot of trouble here with train robbers. They attacked the Wichita run. Kristina was on the train and barely escaped alive, but they killed a whole bunch of people, including Deputy Wade. You know how many kids that poor man has?*
>
> *Anyway, Sheriff Brody is a good guy, but he can't run this town with only one deputy, and the violence is escalating. Rebecca Spencer's shop was fire-bombed, and there was an attempted jailbreak.*
>
> *Sheriff Brody asked me to write and see if you would come home. He's been running ads all year, but so far, no one seems interested. I know you didn't plan to come back, but it's been five years, and we really need you. Would you please consider returning? Maybe being a local lawman isn't as exciting as chasing bandits all over the mountains, but it would be a steady job with decent pay. Please consider.*
>
> *Wes*

Jesse pondered how stressed his friend must have been to write such a terse and jumbled letter. Train robbers attacking the Wichita run? He hoped Allison Spenser's father hadn't been hurt. His thoughts turned to the fourth of their childhood band of troublemakers. Like Lily, Allie was a blond, but she was no ethereal creature; tall and curvy to the point of plumpness, Allie had always been solid and strong. *I wonder if she and Wes got married yet. Probably. They were so in love. Bet they have a whole litter of little Fultons, in spite of Wes's horrible mother.* And still, in her last letter, Kristina hadn't mentioned them. How odd. *Well, she hates gossip, but this isn't gossip, it's news.* Shrugging over his incomprehensible friend, Jesse abandoned the line of questioning and returned to Wes's job offer.

How should he answer the letter? Should he go home, back to the flat prairie and the endless wind? No matter how he wandered, no matter how he hated it,

Garden was home. It still called to him. Not to mention a steady paycheck and a comfortable bed to sleep in would be welcome. *You're getting soft, old man.*

Deciding to put the idea of returning home on the back burner for a while, he ripped open the third envelope.

Jesse,
I hope you'll forgive me for disturbing you. We must talk, as soon as possible. Please come to my aunt's house this Sunday at nine. It's urgent.
Addie

This missive puzzled Jesse more than the other two put together. He wondered if she was not getting along with her aunt or something. *Though if there was any trouble between them, wouldn't Beth have mentioned it?* Try though he might, Jesse couldn't imagine what was going on. *Guess I'll find out Sunday.*

Chapter 12

Addie sat in the rocking chair beside the fire, her knitting needles flying. While Beth could construct the most intricate quilts, all the cutting and stitching drove Addie to distraction. When she wanted to busy her fingers with a task and free her mind, yarn called to her. She'd bought the white skein and a mint green one and was candy striping a blanket. The tiny size of the piece—just long enough to wrap an infant in—warmed her even as it frightened her.

No regrets. Everything is going to be fine. I have to believe that. Thank you, God, for Aunt Beth.

Sitting, her expanding abdomen bulged much more obviously than standing, the slight weight and pressure noticeable. She touched the tiny curve. *Soon Jesse will be here. I want to see him. I hope he agrees that us being together again will be okay.*

She switched from knit to purl stitch to complete the row, creating a recessed bar to contrast with the raised one and let her imagination float away. She saw herself lying on a bed, her baby cuddled in her arms. Behind her, Jesse leaned up on one elbow to look over her body, admiring their child. The image was so vivid she could almost feel it.

A knocking at the door shattered her concentration. She jumped, dropping the partially completed blanket onto the floor. Rising, she called, "Who is it?"

"Addie?" Jesse's warm, familiar voice cut through her, bringing tears to her eyes.

She drew in a deep breath and answered, "Come in."

The door opened and Jesse stepped into the room, the sunlight sparkling through the window turned his pale hair to rich gold and the stubble on his chin gleamed. Unable to stop herself, she took one step towards him and then another until she all but ran across the room, throwing herself into his arms. Shuddering, gulping on sobs, Addie tried desperately to hold back her tears.

"What's wrong, honey?" Jesse asked. "Did something happen?" He tucked his knuckle under her chin and lifted her head, staring down into her eyes.

"You might say that," she replied, hysterical giggles burbling up in her. "Come sit down." She led him to the sofa. "Would you like some coffee?"

"No thanks, Addie," Jesse said, sinking onto the warm brown upholstery.

She settled beside him, even more uncomfortably aware of the firm, outward pressure on her belly. *Be calm, Addie. You know people can't see it yet.* She grasped Jesse's hand and laced his fingers through hers.

He leveled a strange look on her. "Addie, what are you doing?"

"I... we have a problem, Jesse," she said. Then she took a deep breath.

He lowered his eyebrows, his forehead crinkling, the corners of his mouth pinching. "Did someone start a rumor?"

If only... "Not yet, but it's only a matter of time."

Now Jesse really looked confused. "I think you'd better just spell it out for me, Addie. What are you talking about?"

That's right, Addie. Get to it. "Jesse, I... we..." she stuttered, and at last blurted, "We're... we're expecting a baby."

Jesse closed his eyes. "Are you sure?"

"If you open your eyes and look at me, you should be able to see."

He did and the color drained from his face as he took in the changes. Not so much the tiny thickening of her waist, but the swollen breasts that strained the buttons of her shirtwaist. He reached out one tentative hand and gently touched the seam. His eyes seemed to glaze over as though his thoughts were far away.

"Expecting a baby... expecting a baby... expecting a baby..." Addie's words echoed inside his mind as though his head were empty as a tomb.

Dear Lord, why did I not guess? It all made such perfect, terrible sense. The letter. The timing. *Well, man, now what? What are you going to do?*

He knew the answer before his mind even raised the question. *I cannot allow Addie to be hurt any further by my actions, and now there's a little one to consider as well.*

He pictured a little girl with big brown eyes, hiding in the fold of Addie's skirts and his heart clenched. Then he imagined a small boy with golden hair sitting in front of him on Mercury's back and his heart melted. *A little one. Oh Lord in heaven, I'm a father.* While blind panic left him blinking dumbly at the fire, a sense of sparkling warmth spread through him. *I'm a father!*

Jesse met Addie's eyes, and she could see his worry and strain. "How long have you known?"

"Uh…" her voice broke and she cleared her throat. "I've suspected for a few months… maybe three? But I was sure a month ago."

"A month?" he exclaimed, staring at her. "Addie, you've known you were in a family way for a month and you didn't try to contact me?"

"I didn't know where you were." Addie cast her eyes downward. "Beth only told me earlier in the week, when I had to admit… everything to her. I kept hoping if I pretended long enough, it would go away. I guess I wasn't thinking straight."

"I guess not," he said, and the anger in his voice forced her gaze back to his face. "If you'd told me sooner, we might have been able to take care of business before the timing became impossible. Now, no matter what, people will know."

"Well, if I'd known you were nearby…"

"Okay, okay." Jesse sighed. "I wasn't thinking right either. Otherwise, I would have prevented this from happening in the first place. We should have… right away… but…." His face flushed and he took a deep breath. "I guess it's too late to worry about that. Now we have to make it right going forward." He laced his fingers through hers and stroked her skin.

"You mean you want us to…" Hope blossomed. Though she'd felt certain he would take responsible action where she was concerned, her heart had doubted. She hadn't quite dared believe it in her soul.

"Of course, Addie. I put you in this position and it's my duty to make sure you don't suffer for it. No more than necessary."

"Duty and suffering? Is that all you see in this situation?" she asked, hearing the wildness in her own voice.

Jesse sighed. "Not exactly." Suddenly his expression turned vulnerable and he admitted, "Part of me is relieved. I missed you, sweet girl. I like the thought of being with you. I just worry about you, you know? You could have done better."

"I have what I wanted, Jesse," she reassured him. "I have a man I care about, one who cares for me. We'll be all right together. Take care of each other."

He lifted her hand and touched his lips to the sensitive skin on the back. "I think you might be right."

A tear slipped down Addie's cheek. He wiped it away with his thumb. "What's wrong, Addie?"

"I was so scared," she admitted in a whisper.

"My girl? Scared?" He affected a startled expression.

She punched him in the shoulder. "No jokes, Jesse, please."

"All right," he agreed. "No jokes. I get it."

As though sensing she needed more reassurance, he wrapped her in a tight, loving embrace.

If this isn't love, I can't tell the difference. Maybe calling it friendship is his way of protecting himself. Addie leaned her forehead against Jesse's shoulder and allowed the tension to drain from her. Then she lifted her head to meet his eyes.

"Addie, I'm…"

She cut him off with a finger over his lips. "Don't say you're sorry, Jesse. Don't apologize. Please just let this be okay."

He shook his head. "But I *am* sorry, Addie. Sorry I put you in a scary situation. Sorry I tried to walk away. Sorry you spent all these months worrying. I hurt you, Addie. That's the one thing I never wanted to do, and yet it's all I can seem to manage."

The harsh regret in his eyes brought tears to Addie's. *Pregnancy is turning me into a watering pot.*

Poor Jesse, who had defined his life so rigidly that he couldn't accept change even when it was obvious. Who loved her enough to try to spare her from living his misery, and yet couldn't bring himself to admit it. She laid a hand on his cheek and guided his face forward, claiming his lips. "I love you, Jesse, whether you want me to or not. Whether you can accept it or not. You are the heart of my heart and the only man I want. Whatever you are, whatever you are able to give is enough for me, and that's my decision, my choice. You can't choose it for me, can't deny me it."

She kissed him again, cutting off the reply she could see forming in his mind. *I don't want your excuses or your reasons. I don't want your denial. Just let me love you, Jesse West. Just let me be close to you. Let your actions speak since your words are stuck.* She opened her lips, inviting him to kiss her deeper. His tongue surged into her mouth, just as she'd hoped. Her lips curved against his. She slipped her arms around his neck and held him flush against her upper body.

"Addie," he murmured, but it was more an endearment than a comment. She could see he had acquiesced to her urging. He pulled her to stand, still crushing his lips to hers, one arm around her waist, the other petted down her front to feel the slight convexity of her belly. "So little."

"I have a ways to go," she mumbled.

"Not long enough, honey. I should have married you the next day."

"Hush, Jesse. It's in the past. Marry me tomorrow."

"Soon, Addie. I need to make a few arrangements, but I understand how much we need to hurry this."

"And right now?" Addie urged.

"Right now, I'm going to take you to your bed, little Addie, and remind you how good we are together."

She smiled. "I've never forgotten."

He raised one eyebrow. "Do you not want to? Are you feeling sick or something?"

"I think the sickness is waning," she replied, "and I do want to, very much. I've missed touching you, Jesse."

She laced her fingers through his and led him around the sofa and through the room to her bedroom, where she pulled down the covers to reveal the cream-colored sheets beneath her aunt's quilt.

"How cozy," he said as he set to work on the buttons of her blouse. "Looks like a perfect nest for me to lay my sweet lady down in." The garment fell away, leaving only Addie's worn and stretched out chemise covering her breasts. The dark points of her nipples pressed hard against the fabric, clearly visible. Without shame, she thrust her breasts forward, begging Jesse to touch her there.

He lowered the lacy straps on her shoulders, baring her top completely.

"Undress me, Addie," he urged.

She eagerly set to work on his buttons while he reached forward and claimed one aching nipple between his fingertips, before bending down for an arousing suck. Pregnancy had made her breasts sore, and Jesse's touch both hurt and pleased her, but she didn't hold back. Not even when he nipped her before moving to the other side. By that time she had Jesse's shirt on the floor and was working on the buckle of his belt. He released the tapes of her skirt and let it fall. Undergarments quickly followed; both lovers were desperate to be naked. At last, Jesse stepped back and looked Addie all up and down. "I can see it now." He traced his fingers along her belly. "Oh, Addie…"

Stepping close again, she tugged Jesse down onto the bed beside her. He obliged, lifting her breast in one hand so he could suck her again.

"Jesse," she sighed stroking his back. "I'm so glad you're here to stay."

"You'll never be alone again if I can help it, Addie." He mumbled against her belly as he slid his lips over her skin.

Her toes curled in anticipation, knowing where he was headed. She parted her thighs widely so he could access her. Her cheeks heated and a fluttering sensation in her stomach told her anticipation. Jesse kissed her mound and then set to licking her clitoris. One finger and then two invaded her body, making that enticing tickling sensation deep inside her. The dual stimulation had Addie whimpering on the edge of orgasm in no time.

"That's it, Addie, come on," Jesse urged, and the rumbling of his voice against her most sensitive places tipped her over the edge into ecstasy. Her toes curled, gripping the sheets.

Jesse moved to cover her body. Addie tensed, remembering the discomfort of their first coupling. This time was different, however. Jesse slid his erection along the seam of her body, eliciting shivers and shudders from Addie. Her climax, wavering on the edge of dying away, flared to shivering life. Wetness surged, preparing her for Jesse's entry, and he took the invitation, pressing slowly into her shuddering depths. This time the stretching felt wonderful. Filled to her limit, the bulbous head of Jesse's sex bumped and scraped on that magic internal place.

Addie whimpered. She squirmed. Then she let out a shriek as pleasure peaked again.

Jesse couldn't help grinning at Addie. Her uninhibited response pleased him tremendously. As did the lusciousness of her wet, clenching sex. Groaning, he drove deep, pulled back, and drove deep again. Though he kept his movements controlled to ease Addie's transition into sexuality, he didn't stop himself from surging fully into her.

"Jesse," she moaned, her voice soft and breathless.

"Enjoy it, Addie," he urged, knowing she was. "Enjoy me bedding you."

"Oh, Jesse, Jesse…" her whimpering sounded less than coherent, and he realized that in the extremity of her pleasure, she was no longer fully present.

She's fine for the moment, he thought, cupping her bottom with his hands and lifting her so he could plunder her at just the right angle. He dared thrust with a bit more force now that she was completely submerged. Her orgasm was waning, leaving her sex relaxed, wet and submissive to his possession, and he claimed it, claimed every inch, not with force, but with tender insistence. "You're mine, Addie. For all time, you belong to me."

"Hmmmm," she hummed, as though in acquiescence.

Jesse's seed was rising… rising. His own pleasure threatened to break over him. Addie's passage felt so perfectly sweet and wonderful, he couldn't stop the process. Couldn't slow down. *You have a lifetime of tomorrows with this woman, your lover, the mother of your child. You have a lifetime to enjoy her.* The knowledge that his decision had been taken away didn't bother him in the slightest. He pushed deep into his lady and bathed her womb with his seed.

Gasping, Jesse rested a long moment on Addie's body, then, mindful of his weight on her pregnant belly, withdrew and rolled to the side, taking her with him.

With her head cradled on his shoulder, Jesse laced his fingers through Addie's and lifted them both to his mouth, kissing each of her fingers in turn. She settled more comfortably against his shoulder and sighed. "I haven't felt this right in four months."

And that's your fault too, West. You owe this girl so much.

At least now he had the opportunity to repay her for all her sweetness.

Chapter 13

Morning dawned like hope over the little cabin a mile outside of Colorado Springs. Light crept past the mountain peaks and through the pines to wake the couple tucked beneath a thin sheet on a comfortable bed. The man; tall, youthful and muscular, with golden hair, opened his eyes and smiled, pressing a kiss to the auburn hair of a petite and curvy woman, who lay naked in his arms.

"I need to go, Addie," he said.

"No, please stay," she begged.

"I can't, honey." He kissed her again, on the lips this time. "Sooner or later someone will come to buy something. I can't be here alone with you."

Addie rolled onto her front, her arms propped up on Jesse's chest. "We're getting married, right?"

"Of course," he replied.

"And I'm already carrying your baby, almost halfway through. What difference does it make if people gossip? They're going to regardless."

"You're a naughty girl, Addie." He tweaked her nipple. She yelped. "We're going to observe the proprieties. Besides, I need to go back to my room and get some things set up. I think, in a week or so, we'll know better how the future is going to look... Hey, don't make that face at me!" He pulled her down for a sweet kiss. "I'll be with you. I'm marrying you no matter what. The question is where, how, and what the future is going to be like. I have a few details I need to work out."

Addie sighed. "All right then, but be quick about it, Jesse. I sleep much better when you're beside me."

"I know what you mean."

She leaned in for another kiss. Jesse had intended to get up and dress, but the lure of his betrothed's luscious lips was more than he could resist. He grabbed her in a forceful embrace and rolled her under him. Addie squeaked, startled, but offered no protest. In fact, as Jesse took position between her thighs, she hummed in anticipation. Drenched from arousal from the aftermath of a night of fiery lovemaking, his erection slipped easily into the snug embrace of her body.

Now, relaxed and ready, Jesse was able to ride Addie hard. Her expression spoke of the pleasure he was giving her. After holding back for weeks of playful exploration, and then months of separation, Jesse couldn't get enough of Addie's silken depths. *You don't have to, now.* He smiled at the thought.

She pushed up to meet his punishing thrusts, as lost in the moment as he was.

The orgasm that followed was just as hard and wild as the lovemaking had been. Addie and Jesse shuddered together as ecstasy washed over them. "I love you," she murmured.

Jesse pressed one last kiss on her lips and strode to her commode for a quick wash before donning his clothing and leaving the cabin. Addie had fallen back to sleep, done in by a long night of loving.

All the way back to the rooming house where he was staying, his mind dwelt on Addie. On the second chance he had with the girl. *No, she isn't Lily, but she's enough all on her own. I don't need to feel that I've been in any way let down. My future wife is a passionate, beautiful girl with a good head on her shoulders. I could do much worse. Now to figure out how to provide for her without leaving her alone all the time.* The thought caused his shoulders to tense. His love of the wild and dangerous lifestyle bordered on an addiction. How could he settle into life in one town, working day in and day out under someone else's supervision? How could he resist the lure of the open road?

For Addie... and our child... I need to find a way. Mercury snorted, wresting Jesse back to reality. *Pay attention to the road, Jesse.*

Reining in a bit, he slowed his pace and watched the gravel path for dangers. *If only the pitfalls in the future could be so easily detected.* There were so many options open to him, and he didn't know what would work best. In some ways, accepting Wesley Fulton's invitation to return home would be ideal. If the new sheriff accepted Jesse, he could have some of the thrills and excitement of his current life, along with retaining his sense of being a lawman, a servant of justice. That appealed.

He could also catch up with his friends again. *Wes, Kristina, and Allie. Allie's sister the beautiful Miss Rebecca. James Heitschmidt, Kristina's dad, who was like a second father to me. The Spencer parents.* He'd missed them more than he wanted to admit, but going back would be heart-wrenching. Every building in the town carried a memory of Lily, his sweet, lost flower. He could still see in his mind's eye, her golden beauty, her angelic smile. Though the years-old images had faded like photographs, the feelings remained.

I will love Lily until the day I die. That alone would be reason enough not to go back, not because of himself, exactly, but because of Addie. The girl he'd fought attraction for, unsuccessfully. The girl who carried his child. For her, he should consider a different path. Maybe in this town, where her last remaining family member lived, where she'd begun to make a life for herself. He should ask the sheriff, see if there was a deputy position here. Or something else. Could he do it? Work at the mercantile? The livery stable? The hotel? All the thoughts made him wince.

I intend to do right by Addie and the baby, but do I have to do it this way? Really? Jesse was a man who craved open sky. The thought of town life made him itchy enough without the boredom of spending his life placing cans of peaches on shelves.

I should ask Addie what she wants, he decided. *There's no way a woman as independent as her would want to be left out of this process.*

At last satisfied he had an answer that worked, Jesse shook his reins and sent Mercury off in a new direction, towards town. He had a few questions to ask. It wouldn't do to present his lady with choices if he didn't really know what they were.

Addie woke up about an hour later. *Goodness, pregnancy is tiring.* Stretching, she rose from the bed and meandered over to the commode where she regarded her body in the oversized mirror. Curvy as she was, her belly hardly showed yet. *Well, you're not quite halfway. It will be a while before your condition becomes obvious.* She couldn't help smiling. With Jesse on board, everything seemed to be falling into place perfectly, and she had great hopes for her marriage. If passion played any role in the success of a union, they would be just fine.

Whisker burns and love bites dotted her breasts, evidence of an afternoon and evening spent in delicious naughtiness. Her womanly parts ached pleasantly after repeated rounds of lovemaking. *Jesse, darling. I love you so much.* She couldn't feel anything but pleased and proud that he was going to be her husband. *Reluctant husband,* she reminded herself, though the terse thought did little to dampen her joy.

She emptied out the ewer and poured fresh water so she could wash up and dress. She had to set aside two shirts because they would no longer fasten around her breasts. One of her larger ones consented to button and she was able to move forward with her day, brewing coffee and preparing herself a sandwich that would serve as both breakfast and lunch. She sat down to eat, unable to wipe a tender smile from her face.

About an hour later, a loud pounding sounded at the door. Addie, who was washing up a sink full of dishes, drew her eyebrows together in consternation. *I wasn't expecting anyone. Who could be here? Surely Jesse wouldn't be back so soon. Is it a client?* "Who's there?" she called.

"Bear," came the answer.

Addie's whole body tensed. "Just a minute. I'm… indisposed."

Creeping to the entrance with her most silent step, she quickly shot the heavy bolt home. There was no other door in the cabin, and the windows were so small, only an assailant the size of a fox would be able to wriggle through. She was safe for the moment.

"Byron Mills," Addie shouted, letting her anger show in her voice, "you're going too far this time. How dare you come to my home uninvited?"

"C'mon Addie," the growling voice whined. "Open up. I just want to talk."

"I don't like the way you talk, Mills," she replied, not giving an inch. "You manhandled me in a public place. What the hell would I open the door for?"

"You don't need to be so shy now," he insisted. "There's no one around who will be offended, so you can stop playing coy. You want me, Addie. I know you do. Open up. I won't tell anyone. Don't be afraid of my size. I know how to be gentle."

"Compared to what? A tornado? You don't listen well, Mr. Mills. I'm not playing any games. I'm telling you right out that I'm not interested in you. I don't like you, let alone want to be with you, and I don't want you here. Go away. Now."

"Addie!"

"NO!" She yelled, cutting off further comment. "There's nothing to discuss, and I have a rifle aimed at the door. If you don't go away right now, I'm going to see how well it penetrates wood." *Shit, where is the rifle?* She scanned the room, momentarily panicking. "I'm loading the bullets right now, Mills. Get the hell out."

Bear didn't leave. He banged on the door. The whole cabin reverberated with the force of the blow. Paint cracked and flaked, falling to the floor. On a wild hunch, Addie ran into Beth's bedroom and sure enough, the rifle lay across the bureau. Taking a deep breath, she grabbed it and opened the chamber, relieved to see it fully loaded.

The hammering continued unabated.

Addie cocked the weapon and held it ready at her side. Willing her hands to stillness, she drew in a deep breath, centering herself, and opened the bolt that held the door shut. Battered under a barrage of furious blows, the cracking wooden structure swung inward. Bear took a menacing step forward but Addie was ready. She braced the rifle against her shoulder and glared, unblinking.

"Take another step, Mills, and I'll send you to your great-grandparents," Addie snarled. Her finger strained against the trigger as she willed herself not to fire prematurely. "Are you listening?"

To her relief, Bear nodded.

"Good. Now I want you to leave this property and never come back. You are not welcome here. Not even to buy flowers or a quilt for your bed. If I see you on this land again, I'll make sure it's the last thing you do. Don't test me. I assure you I'm serious."

Bear blinked, looking confused as his namesake after waking from hibernation.

"Now scoot before I decide to shoot you on principle." She gestured with the gun. He took a step backwards.

She advanced and he retreated again.

"Miss Addie," he said, lifting his hands, palms up, "this isn't necessary."

"It is," Addie insisted. "Get. Go on." She gestured again.

"This isn't over, Addie." Bear turned and ambled away, casual as though he didn't have a weapon aimed at his back.

Addie slammed the door shut and locked it again. Dropping her rifle on the floor, she walked to the couch and sank down, burying her face in her hands. A tiny shudder ran through her.

Her hands went automatically to her belly. *What would have happened if he'd gotten in?* As if there was a doubt. The big oaf would have raped her and pretended it was her idea. Of course, that's what Bear Mills would do.

And the baby? Would he have been okay? She had no way of knowing, but the knowledge of Jesse's tiny, helpless child being harmed made her feel ill. Literally. Though her legs wanted to collapse under her, she managed to wobble to the chamber pot before being violently sick.

How long she crouched, retching and weeping, Addie wasn't sure, but it seemed like ages. At last, she managed to gain control of herself enough to crawl to the bed and slip in. She wanted nothing more than to sleep forever.

Despite her exhaustion, sleep eluded Addie. She didn't feel safe in the cabin. *Eventually, the door frame would have splintered. I can't keep Bear out forever.* She shuddered again.

Jesse leaped from Mercury's saddle outside the McCoy flower farm, leaving the horse to nibble the dry summer grass. The horse snorted in disgust and gave Jesse a telling look. Sighing, Jesse led Mercury into the barn, slipped off the saddle and rubbed the horse down. In the warm interior, a gentle-faced cow greeted him with a soft moo. He smiled at the sight of the calf beside her, bumping her belly with his little head. A barn cat meowed. While the animals amused him, Jesse still felt restless. He wanted to see his Addie. Needed to. Not only to take her in his arms again, but also because he had important things to discuss.

Leaving his horse to chew on a serving of dry, sweet hay, he approached the house. Trying the handle, Jesse was startled to find the door bolted against him. He knocked. "Addie," he called, pressing his ear against the door. He heard soft whimpering. "Addie, please let me in, honey," he called.

There was a groan and then a soft shuffling. The door opened to reveal Addie, pale and sick-looking, standing before him. *Her pregnancy stomach must have caught up with her again.* Her legs were shaking, so Jesse dropped his coat on the floor, scooped her into his arms and carried her back into the cabin. The smell in the air told him she'd been sick, just as he'd thought. "Poor Addie," he consoled, sinking onto the sofa. She rested, trembling, against his shoulder. "I thought you were past the sick time."

"I did too," she replied.

"What happened?"

A shudder ran through her. "Oh, Jesse. I was so scared."

He blinked, startled. "Scared? Okay, Addie, what happened?" he repeated.

She didn't answer, but a wet heat spread across the front of his shirt.

Realizing he wasn't going to get anything from her right away, he held her cradled against his chest and petted her back. "Addie, sweet girl, it's okay. I'm here now. Right here with you. I have you."

At last, her shuddering subsided to sniffles. From her safe place in his arms, she seemed to be regaining some of her strength. "It's... do you know Byron Mills?" she blurted out. "I think he lives in the same rooming house as you."

Jesse pondered her words. "I don't think so..."

"He goes by Bear." She sobbed.

"Oh yeah," he replied as realization dawned on him. "That guy. Doesn't seem overly bright. What about him?"

"He..." she gulped. "He's sweet on me, I guess, but he's scary about it. He..."

"He what?" Jesse pressed, not quite sure Bear would ever hurt anyone on purpose. *He's a bit dim, but I doubt he's dangerous.*

"He grabbed my hand once and nearly broke all my fingers. A little while ago he came here, uninvited, and tried to break the door down."

Poor Addie. "I'm sure he wasn't trying to scare you. He's just a big guy and not a very intelligent one. I'm sure he doesn't know his own strength."

Addie shook her head. "I don't think that's it. He's so pushy, won't take no for an answer, and he's threatened me."

She's overwrought, Jesse reminded himself. *She's assuming the worst.* Rather than upset her further by dismissing her concerns, he said, "Do you want me to talk to him? You're my betrothed, not his sweetheart. I should set him straight. That might help."

She shivered and stiffened. "No, Jesse. Please don't do that. He's so volatile. He might get violent with you... or me. I hope, since I ran him off with the rifle, he'll finally figure out I'm not interested."

Jesse nodded. *She's exaggerating, but I'm sure her condition is the reason for it. However, if I run into Bear somewhere, I just might mention, man to man, that Addie isn't available.* "Okay, honey. It won't matter much longer anyway. Soon you'll be my bride and all would-be suitors will have to go away. Which reminds me..." he kissed her forehead. "I have a question to ask you."

"What's that?" She demanded with more intensity than the comment warranted. It seemed she was eager to talk about something other than Bear.

"Where would you like to live?" he asked. "We can stay here if you want. I mean, there's a job available as a teller at the bank." Jesse couldn't help shuddering. Being stuck not only inside a building but in that little cage-like structure counting money all day was quickly becoming his definition of hell.

"I have a hard time imagining you doing that," Addie said, her mouth turning upward on one side.

"I know, but I don't feel right running off all over the countryside and leaving you alone all the time, especially with a baby on the way." He stroked her belly. The other corner of her mouth rose, forming a real smile. "And that brings me to another option," he continued. "Remember I told you about my hometown, Garden City?"

Addie nodded.

"Well they have a new sheriff—new means he's only been there five years, I guess—and he needs a deputy. Apparently, the train robbers did get there and robbed a train, way back in December. One of the deputies was killed, so the sheriff is shorthanded. My friend Wesley Fulton wrote to me, asking if I would come back since they haven't had any luck finding someone to replace the deputy."

"Now that I can see you doing," Addie commented.

"Yeah, everything about it is great for me. A steadier, more secure job, close to my friends."

"Do you have any family there?"

Jesse shook his head. "No, honey. No family anywhere. Not since I was young. My friend Kristina's parents kept an eye on me until I was old enough to be on my own. I mean, her mama passed away a few years back, in a cholera outbreak, but before that, she was like my second mother." Pain lanced through him as an image of Lily—sweating and pale, her already-slender figure thin and wasted—floated up in his mind's eye. He must not have concealed it quickly enough, because Addie reacted, silently touching the corner of his mouth, and then the skin between his eyes. *One thing I love about Addie. She never feels the need to fill the silence.*

"I think that's what we should do," the girl said at last.

"But you don't know anyone there," he reminded her. "You've just left your home and traveled here. Are you sure you want to leave your aunt and go with me to some unknown place?"

"Jesse," she answered in a soft, serious voice, "Beth is a sweet, kind woman, but I've only known her a short time. I suspect she might be in the midst of a serious courtship. I would hate for my needs to interfere with her love, and she might just decide to stay around here if I do. I don't much like this town, Jesse. Apart from Beth, there's no one here I care about. I'd rather go where at least you have friends. Maybe they'll be nice to me... if they don't feel too much loyalty to the girl you loved who passed away." She kissed him on the lips. "What was her name?"

"Lily," he replied, his heart aching at the mere mention.

Addie nodded sadly. "I'm sorry for your suffering, but I'm not sorry to have you in my life."

"You deserve better than this," he growled, suddenly feeling fierce.

"Better than the man I love? The father of my baby? You must be dreaming, Jesse." She kissed him again.

"So you would be willing to try my town? It's flat there, nothing like the mountains," he warned her.

She shrugged. "I've lived in the mountains all my life. Why not try something different?"

"I'm game if you are," he said. "When?"

"Soon," she replied. "Soon as possible... well, after Aunt Beth gets back. I think I should tell her goodbye."

"I agree." Then he noticed Addie still looked strained. "What's wrong, sweeting?"

"I'm just exhausted," she replied. "It's tiring growing a baby, and then the mess with Bear..."

"Come on," he said, lifting her again and carrying her to her bedroom. His nose wrinkled at the stench of vomit coming from the chamber pot, but he didn't say a word. He merely tucked Addie into her bed and slipped in beside her, cuddling her in his arms until at last she relaxed and dozed.

While his intended slept away her fatigue and nervousness, Jesse steeled himself and took the chamber pot outside. *Pregnancy isn't fun. Poor Addie.* The effect her condition had had on her emotions... and on her stomach... filled him with sadness.

I have no regrets. I'm going to be a father and I picked a girl who will be a wonderful mother. Now that his unpleasant burden had been dumped in the woods, he felt better overall. *She should get along just fine in Garden City. Kristina will be nice to her. Allison too. They're such open-hearted ladies, they won't be bothered by her lack of feminine wiles. They're birds of a feather, those three.*

He slipped back into the house and joined Addie on the bed, taking her in his arms again so he could enjoy the warm softness of her lush little body. *No regrets at all. There are such worse futures than being married to a passionate, intelligent and alluring woman.*

Chapter 14

Once again Jesse left before dawn, slipping from the bed with a kiss and a lot of lingering caresses. "I have things I have to do, darlin'," he insisted, and though Addie knew that was true, that he was arranging for their future together, she still clung to him and begged him not to go.

"Hush now, little girl." He kissed her forehead. "Hush. I'll be back tonight."

"What if Bear comes back?" she shuddered.

"Keep the door locked," Jesse replied. "I still need to have a talk with that man. Scaring my girl like that." He shook his head.

"Don't, please, Jesse," Addie begged. "Please just leave him be and get me out of here quickly. I think the man is unhinged. I don't want to consider what he'll do if you confront him." Shudders ran through her. She sounded panicky.

No wonder. She's got protective overwrought new mother instincts.

"Okay, Addie. I'll leave it be." *Unless I happen to run into him. It's not like I won't warn him away from my girl.* "Keep the door locked and work on something that makes you feel relaxed and happy. Didn't I see a baby blanket in the front room?"

That brought a ghost of a smile to her lips. "Yes, that's right."

"Good. Make up a warm blanket to wrap our baby in, Addie. It's not the coldest place, Garden City, but it's always windy there. Our little one will need a blanket, and the ones mothers make are always special." He didn't mention that his own little blanket, the one his mother had made, had finally fallen apart when he was eight. That's how long he'd dragged it around.

She nodded.

"And cook something tasty for yourself to eat. Have a good day, darling. I'll come back tonight and hold you. I promise."

This time her smile seemed more genuine.

Jesse spent the day sending telegrams back and forth. First, he sent one to Wesley, letting his friend know he was interested in the job. The message came back almost instantly.

Great news. Contact Sheriff Dylan Brody. No other candidates. Tense here.

Even for a telegram, that sounded terse. *It's a good thing, too. I'm really getting low on funds. Spending months brooding over my girl and only working when something came up nearby wasn't good for my savings.* He sent another telegram, this time to the sheriff.

Hear you need new deputy. Former G.C. native with 5 yrs exp. Interested?

Rather than hover in the office waiting for a reply, Jesse wandered off down the street, peering into shop windows to keep himself busy. Though bored with the mercantile, he stepped in anyway, as it was the busiest place in town. Examining the cluttered jumble of toiletries, farm implements and foodstuffs, Jesse also eavesdropped on several conversations. Listening in had always been a vital part of his job. He overheard a couple whispering over some soft white fabric and deduced they were expecting. The man's subtle touch on his wife's belly confirmed it, as did her glowing smile.

Two men were having a heated discussion on the subject of wheat seeds, and unless Jesse missed his guess, it would degenerate into name-calling in the near future.

And then he heard a rumbling voice that sounded like a wild animal. "I still can't believe it."

"I know what you mean," another voice seconded. This one sounded oily and weasely, Jesse noted. "That bitch is way too high in the instep. You should take her down a peg."

"Mr. West?" a female voice called and Jesse turned to see the assistant from the telegraph office waving a slip of paper at him.

He retrieved the notice and read, Very interested. Pls. see me at your first chance.

Jesse grinned. *I like it when things come together.*

Addie woke up alone again, but this didn't surprise her. Jesse had arrangements to make, and he said he'd be back. *Spending the night together sounds good.* Her body tingled in hopes of another round of sweet loving. Jesse had a skill that set her on fire. She was more than ready to try again. Rolling to her side, she savored the anticipation of her lover's arms around her. *Even better will be when he's my husband and can lie beside me every night. I can't wait.*

On the other hand, Jesse was so clearly still caught up in his late fiancée. That innocent, unconsummated first love would never truly leave him. While he might respect, care for and desire his wife, she had to admit he'd probably never love her. Not like Lily. *Of course, he didn't seem upset about the baby or having to marry me. Maybe he was looking for an excuse.*

Another thought also occurred to her. Jesse hadn't taken her concerns about Bear very seriously. He seemed to think she was exaggerating the danger. *Typical man. Of course Bear doesn't seem that threatening to you. You don't have anything he wants. You also aren't sheltering something innocent and helpless. Oh, Jesse. I wish you had listened to me.* Well, no matter. They would be leaving soon. She only had to stay on guard for a few more days.

That night, Jesse slipped up to the house under full cover of darkness. He'd spent a productive day and was ready to curl up with Addie for the night. He had a request he wanted to make of her before he made love to her again.

He found her better than he'd left her, sitting up in a rocking chair, dressed in a soft, white nightgown, knitting that pretty green and white blanket. The scent of stew and bread warmed the cabin.

"Hello, love." He kissed her temple.

She tilted toward him. "Hi, Jesse."

"Did you have a good rest of the day?" he asked.

She nodded. "Did you get ahold of the sheriff?"

"Sure did," he replied. "He's interested."

"Of course he is." She grinned. "I had no doubt about that. Why wouldn't he? With you on the job, those train robbers will be rounded up in no time."

Jesse couldn't help but smile at her words of encouragement. He kissed her again, on the lips this time. "Is there any food for me here? I'm starving."

"Help yourself."

Jesse squeezed Addie around the shoulders and followed the scent into the kitchen area. A quick rifling of the cupboards produced a bowl into which he ladled rich chicken and vegetable stew. The aroma of marjoram and onions floated up to his nose. He inhaled deeply and smiled. The bread sitting on a cutting board enticed him with its equally savory scent. He spread a thick pat of butter over the surface and carried it to the table. Sinking into a hard, high-backed chair, he took a large bite and savored tender potato and peas. "Mmmm. Addie, this is delicious."

"Thank you." He felt no surprise at her smirk.

"I can't wait to enjoy your cooking every day."

Addie beamed.

Jesse enjoyed a few more bites of his meal before he asked his question. "Are you set on getting married here, Addie?"

"It doesn't matter where. I see you have an interest in doing it over in your hometown. Is that right?"

He nodded. "Well guessed. It's… one of my closest friends, Kristina Heitschmidt. She's a musician. If she could do the music… and maybe her father, James, he can perform weddings. He was sort of like a father to me…though with a new pastor, he might not be interested…"

"It's fine, Jesse," Addie told him, cutting off his gush with a smile. "It's fine."

He grinned at his own exuberance. This was going to be an amazing night.

Chapter 15

Addie puttered around the cabin, wondering what she should do. Two days until Aunt Beth was due home; therefore, at least a day too soon to pack. *If I do it now, I'll be digging everything out before I can even get underway.* Jesse had bought her a carpet bag, which was waiting on top of the trunk at the foot of her bed. He'd bought train tickets yesterday. Somehow, unlike her previous adventure to bring her here, she was looking forward not only to the journey but to the relocation itself.

There's no reason why you should feel such hope. Garden City is probably like every other small town. Full of gossips and busybodies. And yet, this time Jesse would be with her. *To stay. My husband!* She laid both hands on her belly and twirled around the room, her mind on a new skirt and a handful of roses. *Maybe some cake and coffee, and then...* Her smile turned naughty.

So intent was Addie on her happy thoughts, she didn't hear the soft sound of the door slowly swinging open. Not until the hinges hit their sticky spot and screeched.

She whirled, her hand fluttering near her throat. A massive creature of darkness blocked out the daylight filtering in the door.

"Miss Addie," Bear began, taking a step her direction.

Addie scanned the room, looking for the rifle. Panic-stricken, she couldn't remember where she'd put it last. She moved cautiously away from the man.

"Bear Mills, you have a lot of nerve," she said, schooling her voice to disapproving iciness. "Get the hell out of this house."

"Language, Addie," the man tutted. "That's another thing you're going to have to work on. Can't have a wife with a dirty mouth."

"You can't have me for a wife at all!" she retorted, taking another step backwards. Now clear of the couch, she had to find a way past Bear to the door. *Being trapped in the cabin with him can't possibly end well.*

"Now, Addie," he said, taking another heavy step in her direction, "that's enough of your games. You've toyed with my affections long enough. I was willing to let you play coy, but no more. Here, today, we're settling this."

His words seemed slow and stupid, but the shrewdness in his black eyes told her everything she needed to know. This was not an imbecile, but a trickster, one who played at stupidity in order to get away with mayhem. *I'm in the deepest water of my life.*

Addie drew in the fraying edges of her composure. Panicking would only lead her to make unwise decisions. She inhaled and exhaled deliberately, drawing air steadily into her lungs. Focusing on her heartbeat, she willed the wild pounding into steady beats. *You are one with the earth. Your heart beats with the rhythm of the seasons.*

She didn't remember the rest of the chant her mother had taught her. It fractured. *Why can't I focus? Why could I remain calm with a knife at my throat and not now?* The answer came in a flash. She hadn't been pregnant then. Her calm had been upset by her unsteady moods and occasional nausea. Her body had begun to change, which meant her center had shifted and she couldn't find it.

"It's been settled for ages, Mr. Mills," she drawled, retreating toward the kitchen area. He continued to advance, slowly, but inexorably in her direction. "The reason I keep rejecting your advances is simple. I don't like you. I'm not interested in you and I'm not playing games. I want you out of my life for good, now!"

He slowly shook his head from side to side. "That isn't going to happen, Addie. You belong to me. I've always known it. I can feel it. I know, deep down, you can too."

"You're wrong," she replied, not giving an inch. "Dead wrong." Her back hit the kitchen counter. *Shit. Trapped.* She reached behind herself with one hand, scrabbling for anything she could use to help her.

"You just won't stop your playing, will you, silly girl?" He sounded amused, yet exasperated, like someone watching a child dig in the mud. "Maybe 'cuz you're so young, you don't realize how much you need me. How much you would benefit from my teaching."

"Go to hell," Addie hissed. *There's nothing here. Please, God. Let me find something. Don't let this end this way! Jesse, where are you?*

No one burst in the door to help her, and Bear now stood so close, she could smell the whiskey on his breath. The stench made her gag. *I can't vomit now! Please, no!* But it was too late. Overcome with panic, her stomach rebelled, expelling its contents on the giant's boots. He frowned at the mess and for the first time, his expression matched his eyes.

"What's wrong with you, bitch?" he howled.

"Please, Bear. You're scaring me. Stop," Addie begged, hoping for mercy. She straightened, her hand against her belly, the other going back to the counter, still hoping against hope to find something of use.

Pleasure flared in the beetle black eyes.

This is what he's been after all along. He wants me scared. He likes the fear. Her hand closed around something cool and smooth… and sharp. Feeling her way along the biting surface, she was able to clutch a kitchen knife in her hand, seconds before Bear sank one meaty, stinking paw into her hair.

She was unable to prevent a terrified squeak from escaping.

"You ruined my boots!" he roared in her face. "You're going to pay for that. Now, Addie. Your schooling begins now! I'll teach you to show respect for your husband."

"You are NOT my husband," she screamed.

"I will be." The threat in his face made him look less like a slow and clumsy animal and more like an inhuman monster.

Now you drop your act, you bastard. I saw right through you from the first. Bully. Gritting her back teeth, Addie answered him without reflection. "I love someone else. I'm already betrothed."

"Engagements end every day. This one will too. You will break things off with this man and agree to marry me, and if you refuse, I'll come back again and again until you're increasing. Then they'll force you to, and I won't be pleased about that. You don't want me displeased."

"I'm already increasing, you fool," Addie shrieked.

He froze, clearly not comprehending her words, and then the most frightening expression she'd ever seen tightened down his craggy, hairy face. "Slut," he snarled. "You were meant for me. I'll cut that bastard whelp out of you."

Faster than it seemed possible for a man of his size to move, he yanked a pocketknife from his belt and aimed it in the direction of Addie's belly.

Addie was faster. In a single fluid movement, she turned to the side, The blade caught on her hip, a glancing blow that opened her clothing and cut her skin. As she dodged, she slashed, slicing deep into Bear's extended forearm. Blood flew from both wounds.

Bear roared loud as his namesake, clutching his wounded limb. She stumbled back away from him towards the door, giving herself room to maneuver.

"Bitch!"

"Bitches have teeth," Addie shot back, "and they're relentless in defending their pups. Stay back, Bear, or I'll hang your pelt from my wall."

His eyes narrowed, and she read his intention there. Now, in the moment of truth, she was finally able to center herself, drawing all her scattered wits inward in preparation for a final, desperate attempt to save herself and her unborn child.

Bear tensed his muscles, ready to charge. Addie planted her feet, readying herself for his attack.

Jesse regarded the tiny room in which he'd been living. *Well, up until recently.* He grinned. The clean but fading room with its single lumpy bed couldn't compare to spending the night with Addie. *It doesn't matter whether we lie on clean sheets and feather pillows or a thin blanket on the bare ground. What a girl I've found.*

The strangest sensation washed over Jesse. Affection, enjoyment, friendship, passion. All the pleasure, from the innocent to the frankly sexual, wrapped up in the tiny package that was Adeline McCoy, was all his to enjoy, care for, and nurture for the rest of his life.

The feelings this produced swelled up in him and gushed through his whole being, swirling until he became quite dizzy. *What does it mean?* His grief over Lily's loss still ached like a bad tooth, undiminished by the passage of time, and yet that pain did not dim his affection for his bride-to-be.

Jesse shook his head, trying to clear his unruly thoughts. He didn't know what to make of it all. He only knew he was happy to be on the brink of marrying Addie and felt not one iota of anger for her unexpected pregnancy. *That's because you wanted to be with her anyway, and now you have to. Took the pressure off yourself—now you don't have to make the decision.* He'd been a bit of a coward where Addie was concerned, he admitted to himself, but all that was in the past. Now his feisty, red-headed lady was about to become his wife. *There are worse fates.*

He pulled his carpetbag out from under the bed and began stuffing his clothing into it. He was short on money to stay at the rooming house, and with the first of August approaching, it was time to pay up or move out. He opted to stay with Addie since they were leaving this town anyway. The gossips could all go fly a kite.

There's no hiding the facts anyway. She's starting to look pregnant all the time. He thought back to the previous night when he'd undressed her by the light of the lamp and caressed the growing swell. It struck him with awe, the undeniable evidence of their passion, yet another of the many priceless gifts she'd given him. He'd rewarded her with the tenderest pleasure, making her cry out in ecstasy several times before finally joining their bodies together.

Down boy, he thought, pushing against the sudden erection that strained his jeans. *Packing, Jesse. Think about packing. You can have Addie tonight.*

And he would, too. Tonight. Tomorrow night. Every night. *She'll be my wife.* He smiled and returned to his task.

A few minutes later, a nagging sensation brought him out of his chore. Something seemed to be missing.

The wash, you dunce. He'd had his clothing washed in anticipation of travel, and it was hanging on the line, surely dry after most of the day. Grumbling at the thought of leaving the shade of the room for the heat of the out-of-doors, he clomped down the stairs and exited.

A breath of stale, hot wind stole the air from Jesse's lungs. He inhaled deeply to dispel the momentary choking sensation as he crossed the low stubble of dead grass and dry patches of brown, bare dirt around the side of the structure that had been his living space for the last few months. A three-story edifice, once a stately family home, had now mostly gone to ruin, its paint peeling in flakes of sage green. Several had drifted to the ground to reveal dry, weathered boards beneath. The once-gracious porch listed in a creaking pile of rotting boards.

The place looked like what it was: a rooming house for men without much in the way of resources. Shiftless drifters, mostly. *That's what I was, all those years, only thinking about myself. I made some money, and I made some friends, but mostly I just rode wherever the wind blew me. Maybe I made a difference, helped the cause of justice, but I didn't accomplish anything permanent. There will always be another criminal on the run, another sunset to chase. One day my luck would have run out, but no more.*

At last, I have the chance to accomplish something lasting, something of value, contributing to a town, to a community. Adding my skills to their efforts to keep a little patch of civilization on the vast, untamed prairie safe. With Addie at my

116

side, I can add citizens too. Once upon a time, I wanted that. Once, before dreaming died. Before hope was buried in the little cemetery at the edge of town.

Every day seemed to Jesse to be brimming with new hopes and dreams. Far from dead, the gates to his heart burst open to vibrant life. Where had this upswelling of joy come from? *From Addie. She's like the earth itself, the source of life.* And he loved her.

The thought staggered him. He literally missed his next step and had to grab a rotting porch spindle to stabilize himself.

"You okay, Mr. West?" Josiah Hilliard, the owner's teenage son asked, looking up from a nearby fence he was whitewashing. Jesse waved him away with a smile that felt somewhat less than sincere.

How the hell can I love Addie? I loved Lily. I still love Lily. The uncomplicated adoration he'd always felt for his angel, his perfect lady, had not diminished one iota, but that in no way stopped him from loving Addie with all his heart. He didn't understand what was happening, how it was possible.

Guilt and joy mingled in a strange mixture of unsettling emotions that set his heart churning. *Is it true? Can I truly love another woman?* No, not just any woman, but Addie… Loving her seemed not only possible but inescapable. Setting aside the feelings of guilt and confusion he embraced the joy, as he had embraced the news of Addie's pregnancy. Life changed. Everything changed, but change didn't mean for the worse. Not necessarily. *I'm ready for a change.*

Striding to the clothesline, he began pulling pins, dropping them into a sack hanging from the line, and pulled his stiff, dry garments down. *I can't wait to finish packing.* He grinned. Going home felt right in ways he couldn't explain.

A strange sound in the woods captured his attention. If he didn't know better he would have sworn something big was crashing heedlessly through the undergrowth. *No animal moves like that unless it's in pain.* The sound of twigs snapping was now joined by breathless squeaking. Whatever it was, it was hurting bad. He peered through the trees, trying to see if he was in any danger, only to have a small, red-haired figure burst into the yard and hurl herself at him.

"Addie? What the hell?" he demanded, clutching his lady to his chest.

She grabbed his shirt, gulping and wheezing. He lifted her face. Her cheeks were streaked with tears and fresh ones trailed constantly from the corners of her eyes. Her hair stood on end in places as though it had been crushed.

Somehow the shoulder of her shirtwaist was torn open. A spreading ring of red circled a deep slash through her skirt.

"Addie, what's going on?" he demanded. Her body began shaking hard, so hard he couldn't merely support her. He had to lift her clean off her feet. "Addie, can you try to answer me, sweetheart?"

"The..." she choked on a sob. "The... the house."

"What about the house? What happened?" *Oh God, was there an explosion?*

She began to babble a string of incoherent words, in which only two registered on Jesse's senses. 'Bear' and 'knife.'

"Whoa, honey," he insisted. "Did you say Bear came to your house with a knife?"

Addie nodded wildly.

"Are you okay? Did he cut you?"

She nodded again.

"Aw, shit." *Now, what do I do?* "Addie?" Her eyelids fluttered, as though she was about to pass out. Jesse patted her cheek with a bit more force than he liked.

At the sting, Addie's eyes flew open and she shoved at his fingers. He moved to her cut, pressing with the heel of his hand in an attempt to stop the bleeding. She hissed and winced at the pain. "Addie, did Bear hurt you anywhere else? Did he..." The words refused to come out. Even the thought of what he didn't want to say seemed to tighten his throat.

"He threatened me. Threatened to..." she gagged and Jesse moved her away from him slightly, knowing what was coming. He supported her while she emptied her stomach, and then half-carried, half-dragged her away from the mess. Addie took several unsteady breaths and then visibly seemed to be forcing herself under control.

"He grabbed me by the hair and tried to force me to end my engagement with you and then he threatened to cut the baby out of me."

Baby? "How did he know about the baby? Did he undress you?" Her shredded clothing worried him greatly.

She shook her head. "I didn't let him."

"Is he still there, Addie?"

"Yeeeees," she broke off in a whimper.

"I'm going to deal with him. I'm going right now. No one roughs up my girl."

He whipped his pistol out of its holster and made sure it was loaded. If that bastard was anywhere near Beth's house, he wasn't going to see the light of day.

"Go… ing?" Addie burst into hysterical laughter moments before she fainted dead away.

"Damn," Jesse cursed. Scooping his lady into his arms, he carried her into the parlor of the rooming house. Taking a seat on a threadbare red brocade sofa with heavily scarred arms, Jesse cradled Addie's cheek against his shoulder and rubbed her back in slow circles. At last, she stirred, shaking her head fitfully from side to side.

"Addie, honey are you back with me?" he asked.

She started violently, almost knocking herself to the floor.

What on earth could have happened to upset Addie so badly? She's a sturdy girl. Her growing hysteria worried him. *Is this the girl who faced down a knife-wielding bandit? What the hell is going on?*

"Hush, now, Addie. Calm down. It's Jesse. I've got you."

"Jesse?" She sounded so lost.

"Yes, love. I'm right here. Can you tell me what happened?"

She drew in a shuddering breath and began, "Bear came to the cabin and walked right in. I didn't have the door locked."

"I understand. It's rarely locked, isn't that right?" He wanted to be sure she knew he wasn't upset about that.

"Not during the daytime. He threatened me, tried to force me to agree to marry him."

She shivered and Jesse pulled her a little tighter against him.

"When I refused, he became violent, pulling my hair and threatening me with a knife."

"Oh, Addie," Jesse exclaimed. While he knew she had been cut, he'd been hoping it was an accident.

"I know. He said he was going to cut the baby out of me." She sobbed. "I couldn't let him do that."

"Of course not, honey."

Addie was beginning to hyperventilate. Fearing she would pass out again, Jesse cupped her face in his hands and looked into her eyes. "Breathe, Addie. You need to remember to breathe."

He reminded her with slow respirations until she seemed calmer again.

"Did he assault you?" Jesse asked at last. So far, while he could see her experience had been upsetting, it was no worse than the time she'd been grabbed by the bandit, and she hadn't reacted this badly. *She wasn't pregnant then though.*

"I grabbed a kitchen knife," she said.

He nodded his approval. "Good. So you ran him off, or did you just get past him and come to me?"

"Neither." A whimper swallowed her words. Bravely she pushed on, struggling to speak. "He rushed me with his own knife… I… I cut his throat. He's dead, Jesse."

For a moment the world seemed to stop spinning. Jesse's breath caught in his throat. Even his heart ceased to beat. It restarted with an uncomfortable thump and he gasped. "Addie, what?"

"I killed him." She began to cry.

Jesse's thoughts began whirling. *Addie killed someone? My Addie cut a man's throat? How is that even possible? She must be mistaken. She must have scratched him and run away. I mean, she's a capable girl, but she is still a girl. What girl could take down a hulk of a man like Bear Mills? I need to get to the bottom of this.* "Is he still there?"

She lifted her head and stared in disbelief. "Of course he is. He's dead. I can't move him. Where else would he be?" By the end, she was shrieking.

"Calm down, Addie. Calm down. It's okay. You're okay. I'll just head over there and see what's what." He ran his fingers up and down her back.

"I killed him, Jesse. They'll string me up. I murdered a man." She whimpered.

"Addie, if you defended yourself against an attack, that's not murder, honey." *How many men have I killed… have I brought to justice knowing they would be hanged. Taking a life never gets easier. Pray God it never does.* Now his sweetheart had to cope with that very thing. *I should have protected her, dammit. I should have been the one to do this for her. What's one more death on my soul? But not my Addie. She's already suffered too much.*

Unable to stop his insanely circling thoughts, he blurted out, "I need to go there. I'll take a look at the situation and contact the sheriff. I'll make sure you're safe, sweet girl. Will you trust me?"

She looked into his eyes, and he could see her soul bleeding. Her leg, thankfully, seemed to have stopped. "Don't leave me, Jesse."

"You won't be alone, I swear. Mrs. Hilliard! Josiah!"

In answer to his shout, the pounding of feet sounded on the echoing floorboards. "Don't tell them anything, Addie. Not a word. I'll take care of everything."

Hard as Addie was crying, it didn't look like she'd be able to say anything anyway.

"What's going on, Mr. West?" The careworn caretaker of the rooming house pattered into the room, followed by her teenage son. He rose at her entry.

"I'm not sure," he replied. "Something happened at the McCoy cabin. Until I'm sure it's safe, I can't let my intended go back there. Can the two of you please stay with her until I get back? Try not to upset her with a lot of questions. I'll let you know what happened as soon as I return."

Blinking at the rapid delivery of instructions, the woman could only nod. Jesse turned back to Addie, taking her hands in his. "Sweetheart, Mrs. Hilliard is going to sit with you, and Josiah will make sure you're safe. Just try to calm down. I'll take care of everything. Okay?"

Addie just cried.

Jesse hugged her tight. "I love you," he murmured in her ear before rising and leaving the rooming house. He didn't bother saddling Mercury, just swung onto the horse's bare back the way Addie liked to do and rode out down the narrow path toward the cabin.

Chapter 16

Addie cried a while longer, vaguely aware of Mrs. Hilliard milling around the room, fluffing stained sofa pillows and whisking dust off end tables. At last, as the terrified girl began to calm—which in this case meant running out of strength to cry any longer—she began to be more aware of the room. The hulking shape of Josiah Hilliard standing by the door almost seemed threatening, until the sun streaming past the faded draperies revealed a babyface thick with pimples and a chin which had barely learned to sprout stubble. Though physically imposing, he was clearly a boy, not a man.

Addie took several deep breaths and tried to contain herself. Her crying jag had left her feeling numb, though a bit fragile.

"Are you better now, miss?" the landlady asked, extending a handkerchief. Though mended in several places, the scrap of fabric was scrupulously clean. Addie wiped her eyes.

"A bit, I suppose," she said. "I've had a terrible shock, and…" she broke off, remembering too late that her pregnancy was not yet open for discussion, but it was too late. Mrs. Hilliard had already seen her free hand move in the vicinity of her belly. She nodded, but her expression turned stern.

"We're getting married," Addie insisted, "as soon as Aunt Beth comes home."

"See that you do," Mrs. Hilliard replied. Without another word, she swept from the room. Addie almost felt relieved at the older woman's prudishness. It meant she wouldn't be bothered with a passel of irritating questions. Curling into a ball on the sofa, she stared out the window, wondering what would happen next.

Jesse gawked in speechless amazement at the gory spectacle laid out in the kitchen of Elizabeth McCoy's cabin.

As Addie had said, Bear Mills lay contorted on the floor, a sharp paring knife stuck into his neck. The pool of blood around the corpse boggled the imagination.

She must have slashed across his throat and then stuck the blade in. What can I do about this? The sheriff will need to know. Someone like Bear goes missing, people are bound to notice, but will they believe it was self-defense? Most people assumed Bear was slow, and they made allowances, but Addie never felt that way.

And he hadn't listened when she tried to tell him either. *For shame, Jesse.*

Walking away from the carnage, he returned to his horse and began the ride toward town, all the while thinking over to himself how he could present this information without implicating the girl he loved.

Addie sipped a cup of hot tea her unwilling host had presented her. The beverage warmed her insides, but she still remained numb. She'd had no trouble forcing her mind to stillness. Her eyes remained fixed on the window, watching a bright red cardinal hop around the yard, occasionally pecking in the dirt. *I wonder what he's finding out there.*

She longed for the open sky. For the freedom of a bird to come and go and never worry about what others might think. *Life was better when Jesse and I were on the move alone together. I don't know if I'll ever settle completely into town life.* With all he was sacrificing to keep her safe, she had to try. *If I'm not hanged for murder.* The tea sloshed in her belly and threatened to reappear. She swallowed hard.

A clatter of boots and male voices on the stoop alerted her to the fact that Jesse had arrived, and by the sound of it, he'd brought the sheriff with him. Her calm dissolved instantly into a panic. What would she say? What would she do? Her thoughts circled around and around like a dog chasing its tail, and with about as much purpose.

The men clomped into the room and Jessie hurried to Addie's side, setting aside the cup and placing their hands on her leg to hide the bloodstain.

"Addie, I hope you're okay, sweetie. I got the sheriff like I said I would, and I showed him what we saw at your aunt's cabin after I walked you home."

Addie met his eyes with her own wide, confused ones.

"Sorry, Sheriff," Jesse said. "She's still in shock. Here we thought our biggest problem was getting her home without people realizing we'd been alone to-gether, and then … that happened. Poor darling. I can't imagine what must be going through her pretty head right now. No lady should ever have to witness such ugliness."

What the hell is he talking about? That's not what happened! She lowered her eyebrows in question and Jesse made a quick face at her, a stern one. *He's protecting me,* she suddenly realized. *He's choosing words that are true to lie. I am in shock. We were alone together, and we did think our biggest problem was people finding out, and then this happened.*

"So y'all came home from... being alone together, and found Bear Mills dead on the floor?"

"Mmmm," Jesse replied, a hum which the sheriff clearly took for an affirmation, though Addie noted how neutral it sounded. "Imagine my shock walking through the door and finding him like that. Poor Addie."

"So you brought her back here before you came for me? I would have preferred to be notified first."

"Sorry," Jesse replied, looking contrite. "Yes, I brought her into this very room and then went and got you. I didn't know what else to do. I had to be sure Addie was someplace safe. She's my priority now. She and..." He trailed off but glanced at her belly.

Addie blushed. She could feel the heat right to the roots of her hair.

"Oh, Lord have mercy!" the sheriff exclaimed, bumping his forehead with the heel of his hand. "What the hell was Bear doing up there anyway."

"He was looking for me," Addie replied, though she couldn't quite steady her voice. "He seemed to think we were courting no matter what I said. I ran him off once before."

Jesse gave her a hard, questioning look. She returned one that begged him to trust her judgment. He tilted his chin almost imperceptibly.

"Yeah, I know about that," the sheriff replied.

"You do?" Addie turned and stared.

"Well sure, Miz McCoy. As much as he talked about you, I knew he was sweet on you, and as many times as you bluntly told him no, I knew you weren't interested." He eyed her again. "From the look of you, I'd guess you were increasing before you even arrived in town. That right?"

"Yes," Addie replied, "though I don't know why it matters."

"Just trying to establish the facts," he replied. "No wonder you weren't interested in Bear."

"Sheriff, I wasn't interested in Bear because he doesn't appeal to me. He's too bossy and more than a little scary."

"Aw, c'mon. Bear's harmless. It's a shame what happened. I suppose he walked in on a burglar or something."

An image of Bear floated up in Addie's mind, looming over her, big hands grabbing, gagging on blood as she drove the knife into his already slashed jugular vein. She retched.

"Easy, honey," Jesse said in a soothing voice. "I know it's a terrible thing to have seen. I'm sorry you saw it, but try not to panic, Addie. Everything will be okay." He patted her hand.

Addie sighed, trying to release the tension in her shoulders.

"Can anyone confirm your story?" the sheriff asked.

"Probably the Hilliards," Jesse replied. "Josiah has seen me here and there, but I'm sure he didn't see Addie. We're... cautious."

The sheriff made a face, but Addie could see the story made sense to him. *It sounds terribly plausible.*

"Well, folks, I don't suppose we'll ever solve this one. Some crazy drifter must have been wandering through. Bear was in the wrong place at the wrong time. Poor boy never could do anything right. Sorry you had to see that, ma'am."

"Thank you," Addie replied in a tiny voice. Tears were threatening to push their way out of her again.

"I'll send the undertaker to get the body. Give him some time to work. I'm sure you don't want to come back too soon."

Addie nodded. The sheriff plopped his hat back on his head, tipped the brim, and stalked out.

She sagged against Jesse's shoulder. "I thought I was dead."

He shook his head. "Even if you'd confessed, who would believe a little slip of a girl like you taking down a man as big as that? I doubt you were ever in any danger from the law, and in my mind, self-defense is justifiable. Especially with a baby on the way."

Addie swallowed hard. Her eyes felt heavy and dry. Her throat and leg hurt.

Jesse must have seen the weariness stealing over her. He swept her up into his arms and carried her up the stairs to his room.

"Jesse, someone will see!" she protested, but weakly.

"I don't give a damn," he replied. "What difference does it make now?"

He locked the door behind them and set her down on the bed, crouching to remove her shoes before cuddling up beside her.

"I won't be able to sleep," she insisted as a huge yawn threatened to split her face. Just before blackness crashed over her, she thought she heard Jesse's dry chuckle.

Chapter 17

"May I ask just what the hell is going on here?" Beth demanded, stomping into Addie's bedroom and glaring at Jesse, who returned her stare with sleepy eyes.

"Morning, Auntie," Addie said sheepishly, holding the blankets up to her chest, though failing to conceal the lacy shoulder straps that revealed she was wearing only a chemise.

"Don't 'morning' me, silly girl," Beth retorted. "It's nearly noon. You two naughty children better get out of there before you cause a scandal."

"Too late," Jesse muttered. Rising from the bed, he grinned inwardly to see Beth's eyes widen as she realized Jesse was only wearing his underwear; a one-piece gray union suit he'd left unbuttoned down most of his chest.

Ironically, though he and Addie had spent the night together, they hadn't made love. After the terror of Bear's attack two days ago, neither had felt much like it. But holding each other to stave off worries and nightmares… that was another story.

"Come on, Beth," Addie said and Jesse was delighted to note that a teasing light had sprung up in her eyes. He hadn't seen her looking so playful since before the incident. "Aren't you coming to us straight from your lover's bed?"

Beth blushed, her embarrassment staining her pale, freckled cheeks crimson. "I'm an old woman. What difference does it make?"

"You're not old," Addie retorted. "Besides, Jesse and I are betrothed, so what difference does it make?"

Beth smiled. "You see? I told you he'd take it well."

"And you were right." Addie reached out and ran her fingers down Jesse's arm. He shivered at the pleasurable tickling sensation.

"So, what scandal did you two stir up while I was away? Did someone catch you? Is the cat out of the bag about the baby?"

"All of those things," Jesse admitted. "But there's more. Can you give us a few minutes to get dressed, and then we'll sit down with you and fill you in?"

Beth nodded. "I suppose. But no sneaking out the window, young man."

"Of course not," Jesse replied.

Addie laughed, and some of the pinched, haunted look faded from the corners of her eyes.

"You must be joking!" Beth gasped, her cup of tea rattling in the saucer, a little splash sloshing out to stain the fabric of her chocolate-colored skirt.

"I wish I were," Addie replied in a harsh, breathy voice. She looked down into her lap, where her hand clutched tight to Jesse's.

"What on earth was Bear thinking?"

"He was thinking he wanted to bed me and could bully me into compliance."

Jesse stroked his thumb over hers as she spoke, trying to help her retain her composure.

"What are people saying about it? Has anyone given you any trouble?" Beth looked from Addie's eyes to Jesse's and back.

Jesse answered. "I implied to the sheriff that Addie was with me and he decided Bear must have interrupted some burglar. No one suspects Addie had anything to do with it, which is all to the best. Though small as she is, no one would really believe she's capable. In her condition, and with everything that she's gone through, between my stupidity and his, I'm glad not to have to deal with a shadow of suspicion. She had every reason to defend herself, from what she told me."

"I did," Addie insisted. "Though I'm not proud to have taken his life, he gave me no choice. I couldn't let him hurt the baby. It makes me mad how everyone keeps insisting he was harmless or misguided."

"I assumed it," Jesse admitted, and Addie narrowed her eyes at him.

"It's the gentleman's code," Beth replied. "Men are always quick to assume other men are fine, have the best intentions and are misunderstood. That women are being hysterical. They don't perceive the danger other men pose, because they don't pose that danger to *them*."

Addie nodded. "I think that must be true."

Jesse made a face. "He just seemed like a slow and rather stupid man."

"That was the impression he cultivated," Addie retorted. "Everyone fell for it."

"I didn't," Beth insisted. "He always seemed evil to me."

"And me," Addie seconded.

"Okay, okay," Jesse said. He held his free hand up in the air. "I'm sorry I didn't listen. You were right."

Addie shook her head. "I feel horrible."

"I know, honey," he said, stroking the hand he was still holding. "No matter how justified, it's terrible to take a life."

She nodded.

"Well, you two," Beth spoke up, changing the subject, "what are your plans? You say you're betrothed. I assume, as far into her pregnancy as Addie is, you're going to do it soon. When and where is the big day going to take place?"

"In the next few days," Addie replied. "We're going to go to Jesse's hometown. His childhood friend is a church organist, and he wants her to play. Also, he's going to interview for a job there, as a sheriff's deputy."

"So you're relocating?"

"Yes, Auntie," Addie replied.

Beth made a face. "I'm sure that's for the best, but I'll miss you."

"I'll miss you too, Auntie. You can always visit though."

Beth's expression turned considering.

"Are you thinking about Bill?" Addie probed.

Beth shot her an evil glare.

"What? Did something go wrong?"

Her aunt sighed, shoulders sagging. "Not wrong exactly. It was like you thought, Addie. He asked me to marry him."

"Wonderful!" Addie jumped from the sofa and crossed to the rocking chair to hug her aunt.

Beth held up her hand in a 'stop' motion. "I said no."

Addie froze in place, her fingers pressed over her mouth. "What? Why?"

"You know why," Beth replied darkly. "I have a reputation as a loose woman. I can't let him damage his career and future with me." She looked down at her hands.

"Beth," Addie told her aunt gently, placing a hand on the woman's shoulder, "he's not stupid. He understands your reputation, and that it's in the past. He's offering you unreserved support."

"He's thinking with his prick," Beth replied crudely.

Even Jesse flinched.

"Bullshit." Addie's grip tightened on Beth's shoulder. "If that was the case, he wouldn't ask you to marry him. He must love you, Beth. If you turned him down because you think it's somehow protecting him, you're a fool. Is he a good man?"

"The best." Beth's expression went far away.

"And do you really want to stay here in this house alone?"

Beth shuddered. "I can feel a difference. I could feel it when I came back, before I found out about Bear. It's not the same house it was."

"Then go. Marry Bill and be an honest, foul-mouthed woman. Nothing wrong with any of that," Addie insisted.

A slow smile spread across Beth's face. "You know, maybe I will. I'll try to sell the house and relocate."

"Good," Addie told her. "Then I won't have to worry about you being alone. Write me a lot, Aunt Beth. Every week. Promise?"

"Of course, Addie," Beth replied. "And you two come visit. I want to see that baby."

With wistful smiles and hugs all around, the young couple gathered up their belongings and Beth escorted them into town to catch the train for Garden City.

Addie stood beside the black, puffing engine of the Santa Fe Rail Line train that would take her to her new home. Though she'd seen bigger engines, there were only a few cars. No need for something more powerful. Smoke belched from the stack and the whistle blew in an earsplitting shriek. An answering scream from the stock car told her Jesse's horse was not too interested in railway travel. She wondered if that proud beast objected to being housed with a herd of smelly pigs.

A few minutes later, her intended arrived and took her arm, escorting her onto a passenger car for the four-hour trip down out of the mountains to the High Plains.

"This is nice," Addie said, scanning the wood trim and aquamarine brocade upholstery of the car. Jesse walked her to a seat and tucked their luggage into the overhead compartment. Addie couldn't tear her eyes away from the window.

So far away from everything I've ever known. I wonder if it can possibly be better. Everywhere I go, I take my uncouth, overly strong, half-Kiowa self with me.

I don't think I'm bad, but most people see that combination and have no further interest in me. Or worse. Thank God for Jesse. I hope he's right about this place.

His hand slipped into hers and squeezed.

You are my rock, Jesse West, and I love you from your prissy manners to your stalwart courage to your perfect golden hair and charming smile. I'm so glad you're mine. She would share him with the memories of Lily. That was no great hardship. *We'll be okay, Jesse and me.* A memory, lost in the darkness and fog of her horrible experience, suddenly popped into her mind. *Did Jesse say he loves me? I think he did, but that makes no sense. He can't love me. He's said so a whole bunch of times.*

Regardless, she loved him, and that would be enough for her. With luck, they could love their child together. *I don't think that will require luck. Jesse will be a wonderful father.*

As she watched, the steep grades and winding curves of the mountains slowly flattened until they were skirting hills and speeding through tunnels, and then even the hills gave way to the utter flatness of the prairie, with its endless, waving grass, tall as a man's shoulder in places.

The pines all but disappeared, replaced by stunted and wind-blasted oaks, short but glowing with greenery. *What a desolate place.* Far off on the distant horizon, a sight she'd rarely seen—an unobstructed view of the blue and cloudless sky—spread out before her, dazzling in its scope. Suddenly Addie felt smaller than she ever had in her life. The endless expanse of grass below and sky above rendered her smaller than a little red ant, and about as significant.

His eye is on the sparrow, but I've never thought about exactly how much like a sparrow I am. One small life in a sea of millions, in this country alone. How vast an array of different peoples are out there, all different colors, races and nations, all jabbering like birds, and all about as important. Right now I'm heading into a town full of people who will someday know me, but in all likelihood, those in the next town over never will, let alone the next state. Just a little sparrow in a wide, wide world. The thought produced a strange, wistful sensation in the vicinity of her heart.

But here, in her own little corner of the vast world, was a man who had chosen her, had made her the center of his life. She smiled, taking in the vista that would soon become normal to her. She had a strange sense that life was holding its breath, waiting for something momentous to happen. *I'm poised on the brink of a new chapter in my life.* She savored the moment. All too soon it would be nothing but adjustments and difficulties, but for now, she could bask in the hope that everything could be as magical as she imagined.

Full dark had fallen by the time they pulled into the Garden City train depot. Addie's first view of her new hometown was that of a dark and silent street, in which small trees and low brick houses seemed to slumber by the light of a huge full moon. Leafy branches whispered in a low wind that seemed to be blowing from every direction at once. The temperature at this lower elevation was warmer, and sweat beaded on Addie's brow as they navigated the streets until they stood at the base of a large brick block on which the words *Occidental Hotel* were barely visible in the soft, silver light.

Jesse led his bride-to-be into the lobby and secured them two rooms. Then he escorted her to hers and left quickly. *New town, time to act right.* He did steal a kiss though.

No worries, Addie thought as she stretched out on the cream-colored sheets of her empty bed. *We'll be married in a day or two. Then all the gossips can mind their own business.*

Tired after such eventful days and so much travel, Addie closed her eyes and fell into a fitful sleep.

Chapter 18

Morning woke Jesse in a blaze of bright sunlight. It filtered through the small hotel room window with an intensity he'd almost forgotten during his years in the mountains. *Home.* He hoped Addie would like it there. He had a feeling it would be their last address.

Rising, he washed at the basin and dressed in a more formal outfit than his usual jeans and plaid shirt. Today he pulled on a pair of black slacks and a button-up shirt, with a bolo tie. Then he crossed the hallway, his boots echoing on the wood of the floors, and knocked discreetly on Addie's door.

"Are you decent, sweetheart?" he called. She opened, dressed in a dove gray skirt with a white shirtwaist and her boots.

"Yes, Jesse," she replied, taking his arm, casting her eyes to the floor. He grinned at her demure expression, as well as the conservative bun restraining her hair. *Like trying to keep fire in a box.*

"Come with me, love. I know a great place to get some breakfast."

"Wait," Addie replied. "Isn't there a restaurant downstairs? I'm sure I saw one last night."

Jesse chuckled. "Yes, there is, but we're not eating there. Remember the name of this place?"

"Occidental Hotel." Addie sounded befuddled. "Why?"

"The nickname is the Accidental Hotel because if you get anything to eat at the restaurant, it would be an accident."

Addie giggled. "Slow?"

"Impossibly," he agreed. "Now, my friend Kristina and I have stayed in touch all these years by letter. She wrote me ages ago that a lady came to town and opened a café. She says everyone goes there. The menu is limited, but the food is hot, fresh and fast. That sounds better to me. Kristina also says the lady makes cakes… you know, for our wedding. So we can save time by doing two things at once."

By the time he finished his speech, they were striding down the red brick street, heading north towards the edge of town. As they walked, they passed the church, with its oversized bell tower. Addie looked up in frank astonishment and then jumped as loud music began bellowing from the interior.

"That would be Kristina now." Jesse smiled.

"Do you want to say hello?" Addie offered as her stomach let out a tremendous growl. She colored.

"It's okay," he replied. "You need to eat. Besides Kristina lives here in town. We can see her any time."

He escorted Addie up the street, passing houses painted in vibrant reds and dusty greens. One white with black shutters. Another lavender with white curtains hanging in the window. Addie seemed to be taking it all in in silence.

"We're here," he said, indicating a wide, two-story square building. "When I was a kid, this was a livery stable. I wonder how the owner got rid of the horse smell."

And sure enough, an enticing fragrance wafting temptingly into the street, redolent with cinnamon and fresh bread. Addie's stomach growled again.

Jesse hurried her inside and regarded the room, disconcerted by the extreme changes that had been wrought in this place since he left. The barn stalls had been removed and the huge open space divided with a wall along which a counter housed a cast iron cash register and a board on which the menu of the day was posted.

Cinnamon roll with coffee
Eggs with toast or roll and coffee

Those were the only options.

"You want the eggs with the cinnamon roll, don't you?" Jesse asked, ushering his intended to a seat near the window, the better to take in the view of the street. The chair rocked a bit. So did the table. Both the furniture and the floor were intentionally uneven. Jesse supposed it added to the charm, but he did hope they wouldn't spill the coffee.

Addie was nodding vigorously in response to the question. Jesse's stomach was also rumbling, so when a plumply pretty dark-haired woman arrived at the table with two brimming cups of coffee, he said, "two of the egg and cinnamon roll plates, please, ma'am."

"Right away," she replied. "Are you two just passing through?"

Jesse glanced at Addie, who was sucking down her coffee as fast as she could.

"Tell ya what, ma'am. My girl is starving. Me too. Bring the food, and I'll tell you the whole story."

She raised her eyebrows, intrigued, and then bustled into the kitchen, returning with a thick, brown plate in each hand. The cinnamon rolls stood tall, fluffy and enticing against the ceramic, and beside them two sunny side up eggs, shiny with butter and heavily sprinkled with salt and pepper. The mingled aromas of a delicious breakfast made Jesse's mouth water. Addie looked about ready to stick her head directly into the food like a wild animal.

The second the plate landed in front of her, she pounced, tearing a generous bite off the roll and popping it in her mouth. Jesse punctured the yolk of his egg and took a bite. Once he'd swallowed it, he turned the proprietress and said, "We're not passing through, Miss…"

"Carré. Lydia Carré."

Jesse nodded in acknowledgment. "Miss Carré. I'm from here. Growing up, I was close friends with Wesley Fulton, Allison Spencer…"

"And Kristina Williams!" the woman exclaimed. "You must be Jesse West. I've heard so much about you!" It seemed Miss Carré was prone to enthusiasm.

"Williams? I don't know any Kristina Williams," Jesse replied.

"Oh, I mean Kristina Heitschmidt, or she was. She got married back in January."

Jesse gaped. "Kristina got married? I'm shocked she didn't tell me!" *Maybe the letter got lost, like her last one. I bet I get a ton of old mail in the next few weeks.*

"Yeah, the new pastor just sort of swept her off her feet. He came in November and they were married before Christmas. Sooooo romantic." Miss Carré sighed. Jesse noticed she moved her hands a lot when she talked.

"Amazing," Jesse mumbled. "I almost can't believe it."

"Why?" Addie asked. The cinnamon roll had disappeared from her plate and her eyes no longer looked quite so wild.

"She's… listen, Addie, don't get me wrong. Kristina is a wonderful person. Kind and talented and strong, but she's… well, she's not exactly pretty."

Addie made a face. "So what? I think, if anyone, a pastor would be able to see beyond such shallow concerns."

"That's exactly what happened, too," Lydia confided. "Just a minute." She hustled into the kitchen and returned with a mug of hot coffee. Without a moment's hesitation, she pulled a chair up to their table and plunked down. "I think it was love at first sight, for Pastor Cody, at least. He took one look at

Kristina, and I swear his tongue was hanging out. She took a little longer to warm up to him, but before long, they were cooing like any lovers and getting caught sparking in the choir loft." Miss Carré's eyes glowed with amusement. "Everyone's laying bets on when the first baby will arrive, but so far, nothing."

Jesse smiled. He noticed Addie was smiling too. "What put that happy look on your face, darlin'?"

"The town accepted him, even though he's new. They accepted him marrying one of the local ladies, and it sounds like, if she's the church organist, she must be pretty well-respected."

"Oh, very much so," the older woman agreed. "Everyone likes Kristina. Well, everyone except Ilse Jackson and her family."

"Ilse? Is that little cat still around?" Jesse exclaimed. "I would have thought she'd be married to a crown prince and living in Europe by now."

Lydia shook her head. "No such luck. She's still here and stirring up gossip as bad as ever. Her sweetheart finally broke things off with her. He'd had enough of her ugly ways."

"So, then, gossips are not popular here?" Addie's face had taken on a hopeful expression.

"Yes and no," Lydia replied thoughtfully. "There are some, of course, and they do spread rumors, but a lot of people just don't pay it any mind. I don't. I know the Williamses and the Fultons don't, and if they're Mr. West's closest friends, you should have no trouble."

Addie nodded.

Jesse seized on another topic that had piqued his curiosity. "What about the Fultons? I assume you mean Wes Fulton. Did he marry Allison Spencer? For some reason, Kristina never wrote to me about them."

"Yeah, that's kind of a sad story. I'm not surprised Kristina kept mum about it. Wesley did marry Allison, but only a couple of days after the pastor and Kristina. He needed Allie's help after his first wife died. He couldn't care for their daughter alone."

"First wife?" *That can't be right! Wes has been engaged to Allie since we figured out what the word meant. How could he have had a first wife? And why didn't he ever tell me any of this?*

"Yeah, her name was Samantha. She was..."

"Crazy!" Jesse shouted. The other few patrons lingering over their coffee turned to stare. "Oh dear Lord, why on earth did Wesley marry Samantha Davis?"

Miss Carré looked into her cup. "There was a lot of gossip, but I don't know the truth, so I won't say. I guess you'll have to ask him yourself."

"All this talk of weddings," Addie interjected, "brings us to the other reason we came to see you today, Miss Carré. Jesse and I are here to get married, along with him maybe joining the sheriff as deputy. I've heard you might be able to make a cake?"

Lydia smiled, but a sadness in her eyes contradicted the curve of her lips. *No wonder. I can't imagine why a pretty, vivacious woman like her is still single. She must be over thirty.*

"Of course I can. When do you need it by?"

"We don't have anything worked out yet," Addie replied. "How soon can you make it?"

"How much cake do you need?" Lydia pressed. "I can't really answer the question until I know that at least."

"Well, I think it's a small group," Jesse said. "The Fultons. Kristina and her husband. The Spencers and Rebecca. James Heitschmidt."

"I'd like you to come too, Miss Carré," Addie said. "You've given me a wonderful introduction to the town and made me feel welcome. I appreciate that."

"So that makes eleven," Lydia said, blushing and smiling. "I can make a cake that small easily at any time. It would only take me one afternoon. I can even make it pretty with two layers, and some fondant flowers. I can probably have one as early as tomorrow if you let me know before noon."

"I think tomorrow might well be perfect," Addie said. "Think we can arrange it, Jesse?"

"Let's find out," he replied. "We need to talk to the pastor. Do you think you'll need something special to wear?"

"It would be nice," Addie said. "My clothes are a bit worn out. Not to mention, they're practical, not festive, but if the expense is too great, that's okay."

"Well, I'll need to talk to the sheriff, too," Jesse said. "I don't mind spending some money on our wedding if I know I have more coming in."

"We'd better get started," Addie said. "We have a lot to get done before noon."

"We sure do," he agreed. "Thank you, Miss Carré." He dropped a couple of coins on the table and led Addie back out into the street. The sun had fully risen while they ate, and the street was growing hotter.

"Summer's a bit daunting on the prairie," Addie commented, wiping her brow. "It's cooler in the mountains."

"You're right," Jesse said. "But sometime in September the leaves will start turning and the birds will fly south. You should see the Arkansas River in the autumn rainy season. What a mighty gush, not like little mountain streams. Good fishing too."

"I will see it," she reminded him, "if all goes well."

"You're right," he agreed. "Well, this is where we'll likely find the sheriff." He gestured to the jail.

Addie shuddered. "Can I wait in the street? I want to take in the town."

Jesse nodded slowly. "I don't think you can get into too much trouble on a public street in daylight," he said in a serious voice.

Addie hit him on the arm. "Don't be dumb, Jesse. I can get into trouble anywhere."

Laughing, he left her and stepped onto a porch of ragged boards, before pulling open the heavy door. Inside, the room consisted of an open space with a desk and three small cells. Jesse recalled sneaking into the jail on a dare when he was a kid. It had looked much bigger then. Scarier too. He could still remember how hard his heart had pounded as he crept into one of the musty, urine-smelling cells to touch the bed. Though nine at the time, part of him had been convinced some unshaven criminal was about to rise up from one of the dark corners and grab him. *Now I'm talking about working in this place. How life keeps on changing.*

He scanned the room again. It looked so much smaller and less frightening than he recalled. In one of the cells, a young man with ragged, unkempt hair glared balefully at the sheriff, who sprawled in a chair, his feet up on the desk, reading the newspaper and ignoring the prisoner.

At the sound of the door swinging shut, the lawman lifted his head. Jesse took in a face that seemed to be about forty—a weathered forty. The skin on the man's stubbled cheeks was leathery and suntanned, and crow's feet adorned the shrewd dark eyes. His black hair had only the tiniest hint of gray at the temples, but stern grooves bracketed the heavily-mustached mouth. His thin lips compressed into a harsh line. The man rose to a towering height, nearly as tall as Bear Mills had been. "Can I help you?"

"I'm Jesse West," Jesse replied. "I contacted you about the deputy position?"

The harsh lines of the man's face sagged in relief. "Thank the Lord you're here, West. I thought I was going to have to deputize Billy Fulton."

"He'd do an enthusiastic job," Jesse pointed out.

"Yeah, but the poor kid is scared of guns. Anyway, West, your telegram and Fulton's endorsement have me intrigued. Tell me a bit about yourself."

"Well," Jesse began, "I've been working the last five years as a bounty hunter…"

Outside, Addie enjoyed the sun on her face. The air smelled sweetly of flowers and the unfamiliar tang of prairie grass. *Summer. New scents. New life. New opportunities.* She smiled. Jesse had been inside the building a long time, but the waiting didn't bore her. She'd found a seat on a wrought-iron bench and was engaged in watching the world go by.

An older couple walked arm in arm, arguing. Something about their tone of voice and posture suggested their quarrel was a game. A middle-aged man with fading strawberry blond hair and freckles was walking with a golden blond woman whose belly curved outward in a tell-tale sign. She reminded Addie of herself; comfortable with silence. No chirping of conversation swirled around them. The source of communication seemed to be the slow stroking of her ungloved hand—adorned with a huge amethyst and a fat gold band—on his thin shirtsleeve.

They're so happy. Isn't that sweet? Watching them, Addie understood something for the first time about the resiliency of the human heart. This couple appeared to be somewhere between their mid-thirties and forties surely. Aunt Beth was older still, nearly fifty. *There's no wrong time to love. Young, middle-aged. I bet even elderly people sometimes fall in love.* She smiled, her love resonating with the love people experienced all over the world, at any time.

The cycle begins again. She touched her belly with wonder, suddenly realizing a bit more deeply what her pregnancy meant. *A new person to love. A new person to love someone.*

She was still smiling and daydreaming when Jesse joined her, wrapping his arms around her and kissing her cheek.

"How did it go?" Addie asked.

"I got the job," he replied calmly.

Addie squealed and turned around, squeezing him tight around the neck.

"Oof," Jesse wheezed. "Addie, don't strangle me."

"Sorry!" She loosened her grip. He kissed her forehead. "Jesse, are you sure this is what you want?"

Jesse nodded. "I'm ready for it," he replied. "I know your dad lived the bounty hunter life until he was too sick to continue, but it was paling on me. The constant wandering. The cold. I grew up in a settled little town, and that way of life has always been with me. I probably knew I'd settle somewhere eventually. Now is the right time. This is the right place, and you're the right woman. I have no regrets, Addie."

Ignoring propriety, she kissed his lips, right there on the street.

"Come on. Let's see if we can find you something pretty to wear tomorrow."

Down the street from the jail, a mercantile bustled with activity. One window displayed the usual assortment of reins, canned goods, toys and the like. The other contained two dress forms on which skillfully assembled calico dresses with clever pleats tempted passersby.

Jesse pushed open the door and walked Addie inside.

The same woman Addie had seen walking down the street sat leaning over a work table, pinning a pattern to a piece of blue checkered fabric. Around her, more fabric hung on the walls, in lieu of wallpaper.

The beautiful blond rose and approached the couple.

"Hello," Addie said, and then she couldn't think of what to say next.

"Hello," the woman replied in a soft, warm voice. "I'm Rebecca Heitschmidt. How can I help you?" She extended her hand.

Jesse seemed to be startled by the name. He stared at the blond as though he had seen a ghost. Then his eyes shot to the mercantile counter, where the freckled man was polishing the shining wooden surface with a red rag.

Addie grasped the woman's hand hesitantly, but the warmth of her welcome overcame Addie's momentary shyness. "Nice to meet you, Rebecca. I'm Addie, and of course, you know Jesse." The woman acknowledged her agreement with a nod and a pretty smile for Jesse. "We're planning a very quick wedding, and I don't have anything pretty and new to wear. Think you can help?"

"Do you have any idea how quick?" Rebecca asked.

"Tomorrow? Maybe the next day."

Rebecca's eyes narrowed, not in anger, but in thought. "It's possible, but it will take some work, and probably alterations on an existing piece. It might take a while. Can we get started right away?"

"We have so many plans to make," Addie complained, then kicked herself for her whiny tone.

"Tell you what," Jesse interjected, "you stay and get something nice. I'll go talk to the pastor and Kristina. Try to organize the rest of the details. Is that okay, Addie? I'll check in soon."

"It's fine," she replied. "Go ahead. I think you'd get bored with dress talk pretty quickly."

Jesse nodded. "You got that right. Take care of my girl, Miss Spencer… uh, Miz Heitschmidt. It's good to see you again." He shook her hand warmly, kissed Addie on the cheek, and meandered out.

Addie giggled and then turned to see Rebecca also smiling. "It's been so long since I saw Jesse, I almost didn't recognize him."

It gave Addie a strange feeling, knowing all the people in this town knew her almost-husband better than she did.

"There's a little something you should know," Addie said, "and I hope you're not one of the gossips in this town."

"Heavens, no!" the woman exclaimed. "I hate gossip."

The vehement answer seemed out of place with Rebecca's calm demeanor, but it made Addie relax, made her willing to trust. "It's going to be hard to fit me for a skirt," Addie said bluntly. "I'm expecting."

Rebecca didn't even raise an eyebrow, which made Addie like her even more. "That might be tricky, but I think I might have a solution. Stay here."

Chapter 19

What to do first? Jesse wondered as he walked. *Maybe the pastor. That will tell us a lot about whether we can do this tomorrow. Maybe Kristina will be there too if they're married.*

Arriving at the church, he pulled open one of the heavy doors and entered. At first, it seemed the building was empty, but then he realized that the front row was occupied by a couple. A strawberry blond woman sat on the lap of a black-haired man, clutching him as they devoured each other's mouths in a wild, indiscreet kiss.

"Ahem." Jesse cleared his throat.

The woman jumped to her feet, her hands pressed to her burning, freckled face.

I know that face. I've known it my whole life!

"Jesse?" No longer embarrassed, she flew to him and hugged him tight.

"Kristina, it's so good to see you!" He returned the embrace. "I've missed you."

"Missed you too!" she squealed.

"And I sure didn't expect to find you sparking with someone. Kristina, really!"

She giggled. "Jesse, this is my husband, Cody Williams."

Jesse regarded the handsome, black-haired man who stood by, looking on in uncertainty at the stranger hugging his wife.

"Reverend," Jesse said, "Kristina and I have been friends since we were babies. Her dad practically raised me, so please pardon the informal greeting."

The young pastor made a face and pulled his wife out of Jesse's arms, hugging her himself. "No harm done, but you'll understand if I don't take too kindly to see someone clutching my Kristina."

"I understand," Jesse said, amused by his jealousy, not to mention his twangy Texas drawl. "I'll keep that in mind." Far from offended, Jesse was overjoyed at how passionately his friend was loved. *Of course, anyone who could get past Kristina's strong personality and stubborn German-ness—and her freckles—would have to love her beyond a mere attraction.*

"What's going on, Jesse?" Kristina asked from her husband's embrace. "You seem like a man on a mission."

"Oh, um…" Suddenly Jesse felt shy. "I need your professional services. Both of you."

Kristina's mouth dropped into a happy gasp, but Cody regarded Jesse coolly.

"I… um… I need to get married." There, he'd said it. "So I need a pastor and a musician. Can you help me out?"

"Sure," Kristina said. "When?"

"Tomorrow?" Jesse suggested.

"I've never known a town like this one," the pastor drawled, "for people wanting to marry on a whim. Hasn't anyone heard of planning a nice wedding?"

"Sorry," Jesse said. "There's no time for that."

Cody furrowed one eyebrow. "Did someone's virtue get compromised?" The glare he focused on Jesse had turned decidedly hostile.

"Thoroughly," Jesse admitted, a hint of sarcasm creeping into his tone in response to the pastor's glower.

"Hey, now, you two!" Kristina wriggled out of Cody's arms and stepped away so she could face both men. "Cody, I love you. You know that. Jesse is my friend, almost like a brother. There's no competition here, stallions, so stop feeling your oats." Both men nailed the tall woman with a stern stare, but she didn't flinch. "I'm not kidding. Stop."

At last, Cody chuckled, and Jesse couldn't help but join him. "That was stupid," the pastor said. "It's just… I've been listening to my wife sing your praises all this time. All the fun you four rascals got into together. I think…" he glanced at Kristina. She looked back, daring him to speak. "I think she might have been sweet on you for a while there. Sorry. I got a little jealous."

Kristina blushed but regarded the men steadily.

"It wasn't precisely a secret," Jesse replied. "But I wasn't right for her. I always knew it. Now I know why." He extended his hand. "I'm glad to meet you, Cody. I'm glad Kristina has a husband who can, at times, be a little jealous. She needs it."

Kristina rolled her eyes. "If the humiliating journey down memory lane is through, gentlemen, I believe we have business to attend to?"

"Sure thing," Cody agreed, visibly fighting a smile. "We can do a quick wedding tomorrow, right, Kris?"

"Of course," Kristina insisted. "But you'll need to talk to Becky and Lydia…"

"We talked to Miss Carré over breakfast, and Addie is with Becky right now." She shook her head. "Mr. Pragmatic West. Have any pieces you want played?"

Jesse shrugged. "I'll ask Addie, but for me, it's whatever you think is fitting."

"Okay," Kristina agreed easily. "If she wants something in particular, let me know. Come find me by the end of the day if you need me to change anything."

"You're an angel, Kristina," Jesse said fervently. "Thank you. And thank you, Reverend Williams."

"Call me Cody," the young man insisted." If you're sort of Kristina's brother, then you're family."

I like this fellow. He's the most relaxed pastor I've ever seen, now that he's stopped competing.

"Well, Jesse, you'd better scoot. I have some practicing to do, and I'm sure you're even busier," Kristina urged. "See you tomorrow."

"I'll be there, with Addie," Jesse insisted.

"I can't wait to meet her," Kristina said, her eyes glowing.

She's happy for me. He risked the pastor's wrath to give his friend another, less intense hug and then walked back out of the church and into the street.

It was too soon to check in on Addie, and so he wandered, trying to take in the changes to the town he'd grown up in, and the things that had stayed the same. Eventually, his aimless wandering led him to the cemetery. Without reflection, he entered the wrought iron gate and stared unseeing over irregular gray stones that seemed to be pushing their way up through the level, grassless soil. So bleak were the colors there that the odd wreath or sprig of dried flowers seemed almost violent in its vibrancy. *Or maybe it's just my eyes.* He closed them for a moment and looked again. Still, the scene seemed to dig straight into his brain, bringing with it strange thoughts.

In some ways, the cemetery is as important to a town as the church or the hotel. Here lies our history, not in ink, but in bone. Here lay Gertrude Heitschmidt, Kristina's mother. A fresher grave held Calvin Heitschmidt, aged 21. Jesse swallowed. He hadn't known the young man had died. What a waste of a promising young life. Another grave. Deputy Wade Charles. Aged 33 years. The death date was the same as for Calvin. Jesse wondered at that. *Did Calvin die in the train robbery? Couldn't be. He's been away for years. Must have been a coincidence.*

At last, under a small but shady aspen tree, a round stone in a gray as somber as sorrow itself bore the name Lily Wilder. Born 1866. Died 1884. Beloved by all. Rest in peace.

Jesse fell to his knees in front of the grave of his first love. The weasels were chewing on his innards again. *What is wrong with me? I'm getting married tomorrow. How can I still be hurting this badly?* And yet there was no denying the tears welling in his eyes. "Lily," he murmured.

"Jesse," a soft female voice said. He looked up, dragging his sleeve across his cheek.

"Kris?" The woman standing above him was none other than Kristina. She knelt beside him and wrapped her arm around his waist.

"Watch it," he joked, "Cody won't like that."

"Cody will understand," she insisted. "He trusts me. Needed to say goodbye?"

He closed his eyes. "I can't. How can I let her go?"

"You don't have to," Kristina said. "She'll always be part of you. She's at peace now, Jesse, and so are you, aren't you? Getting married? Are you and Addie happy together?"

Burning wetness slipped down Jesse's cheek. "I love her."

"That's good, Jesse," Kristina said.

"It's wrong," he retorted, as much in response to his own confused feelings as to Kristina's comment. "How can I love Addie so much and still miss Lily just as if she'd died yesterday?"

"Because you're that kind of man," Kristina replied. "You have a loving heart. I don't think it's any disloyalty to Lily for you to love Addie. In fact, I'm pretty sure Lily would approve. She didn't have a selfish bone in her body. She would want you to be happy, and if it wasn't with her, she wouldn't begrudge you someone else. It doesn't mean you didn't truly love her, or that you're over her. If your Addie is a good woman, she can share your heart with Lily's memory."

"She can. She does."

"Then let it be okay, Jesse. Let yourself care for Addie. Don't deny her your love. You were made to be loved, and you have been. Twice. By good women from the sound of it. That's a blessing, not a problem."

"I had so little time with Lily."

"I know, Jesse. She was a spring blossom. She faded quickly, but what time she was here, you made her really happy. You know you did."

Images danced behind Jesse's eyes. Going for a moonlit walk with Lily because she didn't enjoy the noise and fuss of the barn dance. Sitting beside her in church, their hands discreetly laced together on the pew. Stealing kisses at every opportunity.

Reality refocused into Kristina's freckled face. Tears streamed over the spots and along her snub nose. "You ran away from this," she said. "You didn't let yourself grieve, but that meant you didn't get to enjoy the good memories either. It hurts more if you fight it, Jesse. Don't fight. Let yourself admit how much it hurts to lose someone you love, even if you have the love of others. Those who care will share your pain with you, and your joy."

"You must be the best pastor's wife ever," Jesse said, hugging Kristina tight.

"You're going to be okay, Jesse," she said.

The sun filtered onto his face, warming his skin. A cool breeze tapped gently against his cheek. It felt like a kiss. Jesse looked up into the leafy branches of the aspen and saw a gentle gray dove regarding him with solemn black eyes. It cooed once and then took wing, disappearing into the endless horizon.

He rose, helping Kristina to her feet. "Come on," he said as love and hope burst bright as a prairie sunrise burst in his heart, chasing the darkness and shadows away and leaving him clean. Lily was still there, a warm, wonderful memory of innocent love, but her presence took nothing away from Addie. "I need to go find my girl. Tell her... tell her everything. Tell her how much she means to me."

Kristina smiled through her tears. "I'm so glad you're home, Jesse," she said.

"So am I, Kris," he replied. "So am I."

From his vantage point high on an upper floor of the Occidental Hotel, a silent watcher regarded the streets. A blond man in a dark suit strode, his step buoyant, past the edifice. The watcher ground his teeth, recognizing the man as the one who had raided his hideout months ago. *I will make that bastard pay,* he vowed, *along with this entire damned town.*

He eased the window away from the casement, hoping to hear as well as see. He didn't have long to wait. The man ducked into the general store and returned a moment later with a short, plump, red-haired woman, who clung to his arm.

"Addie, sweetheart, is your new dress going to be ready?" he asked.

"Yes, Jesse," she replied, turning sickly adoring eyes up at her suitor. "How did you do?"

"I'm all set," he replied. "We can do this tomorrow, just like we hoped. Shall we let Lydia know?"

"Oh yes," the woman called Addie replied. "I can't wait. It's hard to believe we're finally getting married, Jesse."

Addie and Jesse. The watcher stored the names away for later use. *They'll be hearing from me again soon.*

"I don't think it's so surprising," Jesse replied. "After all, I love you. I've loved you since... I don't even know when. A long time."

The woman froze. "You mean it, Jesse? But what about..."

"I can love you without forgetting her, right, Addie?" He patted her arm. "Don't get me wrong, she was a good woman, but you're in every way her equal. I'm not sorry we're together. I'm glad. I can't wait for us to be married."

He leaned over and kissed the woman on the forehead.

Even from his vantage point in the window, the watcher could see the girl beaming.

Smile for now, pretty lady. Enjoy your wedding day. Sometime soon, you'll be making my acquaintance, and then, I don't think you'll look so happy anymore.

Grinning, the watcher closed the casement and returned to his room. *This is going to take some serious time and planning, but I will have my revenge.*

Dear Reader,

I hope you enjoyed your journey with Jesse and Addie. Apologies for the tiny cliffhanger, but of course all will be resolved in Book 4, *High Plains Passion*.

This story was particularly enjoyable to write, not only because Jesse is majorly book-boyfriend crushworthy, but because I wrote it for National Novel Writing Month… and I won! NaNoWriMo, if you're not familiar with it, takes place every November. It challenges writers to produce 50,000 words in a month. It's a great opportunity for people who want to write but need a push to receive a boost of motivation through writing tools, connection with other writers, etc.

Okay, enough of that. I'm not a paid sponsor or anything. I just enjoy it the contest and wanted to spread the word.

If you have any questions about the competition, about the series or about me, please feel free to email me at simonebeaudelaireauthor@hotmail.com or connect with me on Facebook, and please, please hop over the Amazon and leave a brief review.

Love always,
Simone

Discover more books by Simone Beaudelaire at
https://www.nextchapter.pub/authors/simone-beaudelaire-romance-author.

Want to know when one of our books is free or discounted for Kindle? Join the newsletter at http://eepurl.com/bqqB3H.

Best regards,
Simone Beaudelaire and the Next Chapter Team

The story continues in *High Plains Passion*.

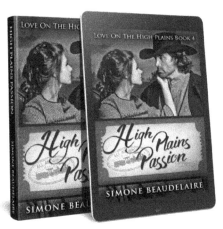

To read the first chapter for free, please head to:
https://www.nextchapter.pub/books/high-plains-passion

Books by Simone Beaudelaire

When the Music Ends (The Hearts in Winter Chronicles Book 1)
When the Words are Spoken (The Hearts in Winter Chronicles Book 2)
Caroline's Choice (The Hearts in Winter Chronicles Book 3)
When the Heart Heals (The Hearts in Winter Chronicles Book 4)
The Naphil's Kiss
Blood Fever
Polar Heat
Xaman (with Edwin Stark)
Darkness Waits (with Edwin Stark)
Watching Over the Watcher
Baylee Breaking
Amor Maldito: Romantic Tragedies from Tejano Folklore
Keeping Katerina (The Victorians Book 1)
Devin's Dilemma (The Victorians Book 2)
Colin's Conundrum (The Victorians Book 3)
High Plains Promise (Love on the High Plains Book 2)
High Plains Heartbreak (Love on the High Plains Book 3)
High Plains Passion (Love on the High Plains Book 4)
Devilfire (American Hauntings Book 1)
Saving Sam (The Wounded Warriors Book 1 with J.M. Northup)
Justifying Jack (The Wounded Warriors Book 2 with J.M. Northup)
Making Mike (The Wounded Warriors Book 3 with J.M Northup)
Si tu m'Aimes (If you Love me)

About the Author

In the world of the written word, Simone Beaudelaire strives for technical excellence while advancing a worldview in which the sacred and the sensual blend into stories of people whose relationships are founded in faith but are no less passionate for it. Unapologetically explicit, yet undeniably classy, Beaudelaire's 20+ novels aim to make readers think, cry, pray… and get a little hot and bothered.

In real life, the author's alter-ego teaches composition at a community college in a small western Kansas town, where she lives with her four children, two cats, and husband—fellow author Edwin Stark.

As both romance writer and academic, Beaudelaire devotes herself to promoting the rhetorical value of the romance in hopes of overcoming the stigma associated with literature's biggest female-centered genre.

Lightning Source UK Ltd.
Milton Keynes UK
UKHW011937030720
366006UK00007B/204

9 781715 098896